APACHE TRAIL #9

BY PAUL LEDD

ZEBRA BOOKS
KENSINGTON PUBLISHING CORP.

ZEBRA BOOKS

are published by

KENSINGTON PUBLISHING CORP.
475 Park Avenue South
New York, N.Y. 10016

Printed in the United States of America

1

The tall man stood in the narrow ribbon of shade cast by the stage stop awning, watching the shimmering, bluish heat waves rise off the red-brown desert. Across the packed earth of the station yard, a stand of withered cottonwoods lined a sandy, parched streambed.

"Nothing?" the voice at his shoulder asked.

Shelter Morgan shook his head, removed his hat, and wiped his forehead with the cuff of his shirt. "Is he usually this late?"

"We've had trouble on the line," the fat man told him. He sighed and returned to the comparative coolness of the stage station. Shelter crouched on his heels, watching, waiting, a blue-eyed, dark-haired man in a faded blue shirt and gray hat. A well-used Colt .44 dangled from his belt. He squinted into the glare of sunlight once again, trying to follow the stage road back toward Fort Bowie, but he saw nothing.

Damn this impatience, damn the squirrel which dug the burrow where his big gray horse mis-stepped and broke its slender leg.

With a sigh Shelter rose and walked to the circular wooden trough across the yard. He rinsed his face in the tepid water, slicked back his dark hair and leaned against the iron-bound trough.

He took the letter from his shirt pocket once again and again read the terse, meaningful message from Sam Rutledge.

"Crater, Arizona. Du Rose here."

It was a hastily scribbled note, and Sam Rutledge had undoubtedly been on the fly when he wrote it. The man had a tough time staying on the right side of the law. A pasteboard sharper, Rutledge was prodded along by the local law on a regular basis. But he was utterly trustworthy in certain ways.

If Rutledge said Du Rose was in Crater, he was.

Shelter looked off across the desert. Still there was nothing to be seen, nothing but a flat, barren expanse of wasteland. He walked to the cottonwood grove and sat on a low growing branch, watching the dry wind rattle the leaves of the ancient trees.

The shadows shifted and blended. The sun began its slow downward arc and still the stage did not come. *Du Rose here.* And how long would he be there? He could already be gone, while Shelter sat at this godforsaken desert outpost watching, only watching.

Du Rose—First Lieutenant Charles Du Rose. First Lieutenant Charles Du Rose squinting over the rifle sights. First Lieutenant Charles Du Rose with an expression of satisfaction and surprise on his dark face as the rifle exploded in his hands and

Welton Williams jerked with the impact of the bullet.

First Lieutenant Charles Du Rose, CSA.

For some reason Du Rose was one of the men he recalled most clearly although they hadn't known each other well. Du Rose had been attached to the staff of General Custis. A narrow, dull-eyed man with straight dark hair which had grown extremely long during the course of the war. Shelter had seen him kick a wounded corporal for not rising and coming to attention. Maybe that was why he remembered that face so well.

You don't forget a man like that—one who is on the brink of sadism. He was a natural for the game.

The war had been shuddering to a bloody halt and Shelter Morgan had been summoned to Colonel Fainer's tent. The camp was on the bloody Conasauga River in Georgia, and death was in the air.

Blackened trees were pasted against the smoky sky. Men fell dead and dying upon the ground. Snow lay in patches beneath the trees.

"Shell," Fainer had greeted him with a smile, standing behind his makeshift desk. The others were already there. Leland Mason, Reg Bowlen, Major Twyner, Du Rose appraising Shelter Morgan with dark eyes.

And in the corner, deep in shadows, was the general himself. It was General Custis who explained what they wanted.

"Gold, Morgan. When we were pushed out of Tennessee, we were pushed fast. We left much behind. We left," the general hesitated, "a quarter of a million dollars in gold, buried near Chicka-mauga.

"I understand you're a Tennessee man," the general said lighting a cigar which curled pale smoke up past his broad face.

"That's right."

"Know that area, do you?"

"I was born in Pikeville. A stone's throw up the creek."

"Good." Custis leaned forward, putting his hands on Fainer's desk. His green eyes glinted in the lantern light and Shelter, waiting, let his eyes sweep over the rest of the gathered officers. They in turn studied Shelter carefully.

"I want you to have a try at bringing that gold through the lines, Morgan," General Custis said finally. "Can it be done? It will mean crossing the enemy lines twice, traveling under cover of darkness, I suppose. Keeping to the hills. Can it be done?"

"Won't know till I try, sir," Shelter said with a slow smile. "But maybe. With a few hand-picked men. Maybe, if we keep to the ridges, with a lot of luck."

"We need that money, Morgan. Need it badly. There's men out there dying with no morphine to ease their pain. There's men out there," he pointed with his cigar, "with no shoes, with no blankets and winter coming on. Our guns are empty, our bellies are empty. It has to be done."

Shelter nodded again. It had to be done, but it was a suicide mission and they knew it. Twice across the Union lines carrying that gold. Not likely. But what Custis said was true enough. They had nothing. They were getting their butts whipped badly, leaving broken, bloody men along the trail to defeat.

So he picked his men, carefully, and in the dead of night, wearing civilian clothes, they slipped out of Georgia. Shelter, Welton Williams, Jeb Thornton, Charles Dinkum, known as the Dink, and the Kentuckian, Bob Keane.

The odds were against it, but they had done it. Suffering indescribable hardship, they had pulled it off. Keane didn't make it back. He had outlined himself against the skyline and a Union sharpshooter took him down. Sergeant Thornton had also been wounded, but Jeb hung on. Hung on until they reached Georgia, riding lathered horses, bringing with them hope for survival in the form of gold dollars.

And then the traitors had ambushed Shelter's men. Cut them down in that clearing. Custis, Fainer, the rest of them. Twenty officers and men with their eyes glittering like gold, their rifles belching smoke. Williams went down in a blaze of glory along with Thornton and Dinkum, and these bloody traitors collected their gold.

But they had made a mistake. They had left a man alive and his name was Shelter Morgan. They had left him alive to hunt them down one by one. He was a man with a long and bitter memory and he remembered them well. The evil dark eyes of Charles Du Rose, First Lieutenant, CSA were prominent in that memory.

A column of dust rose from the Arizona desert

and Shelter stood, squinting into the distance. It was a minute before he could make out the stage and four-horse team.

The driver was putting the lash to those ponies. They streaked on across the salt flats at a dead run despite the heat of late afternoon.

It suited Shelter well enough. He turned back toward the station, gathered up his gear—bedroll, saddle, and Winchester—and stood waiting.

The station manager had seen the dust too. He had a fresh team drawn up in the yard, ready to go. He grumbled a curse and sucked at his lip as he saw the way the horses were being run.

After another minute they could see the coach rolling through the trees, slowing now as it approached the station. A narrow, bearded man with a huge flop hat was in the box. He ya-hooed as the coach swung into the yard, spreading a cloud of yellow dust which slowly settled as the coach rocked to a halt.

"Trying to kill 'em, Windy?" the station manager shouted.

"Better them than me, Jake." The driver didn't step down from the box but the passengers unsteadily clambered down.

"Trouble?" Jake called, unhitching the trace chains.

"You know Hal Pierce?" the driver asked, leaning forward to talk to the man.

"Hell, yes, of course I know him," Jake answered irritably.

"Do you see him?" Windy asked.

"Do I see him?" Jake looked at the stage

passengers, not comprehending. "No, dammit, I don't see him."

"And you won't no more. Hal was riding shotgun with me. Apaches jumped out of those rocks up along Sand Creek. Hal took an arrow in the throat. Now them horses be damned," Windy said, spitting on the flank of the near wheel horse. "I'll run 'em, by God, when I see Chiricahua—and so would you Jake, so would you."

Jake was still grumbling when he led the weary team off to be cooled down by his ancient Mexican helper.

"It was terrible, just terrible, terrible!" The speaker was a blonde woman, short and round with a mountain of curls. "Terrible." The older man who was with her patted her hand.

"It's over now, Bessie."

Shelter nodded to the couple as they passed him, entering the stage station. "Fifteen minutes!" Windy yelled at them. The woman gave the stage driver a cold, piercing glare.

"Got room on top for another man?" Shelter called up.

"Ain't exactly safe up here," Windy said, spitting a stream of tobacco juice.

"So I hear. I'm low on cash, partner. I'll ride shotgun for a free ticket to Crater."

Windy looked the tall man up and down, noticing the easy way the Colt rested on his hip, his cat-like movements. He nodded.

"You've got a deal there, mister. If the company complains I'll pay for your ticket. I can't watch the team and the bushes all at once. Though this is likely to be the shortest job you ever hired on for."

"More Apaches?"

"That ain't the half of it," Windy said with a shake of his head.

"Beats walking," Shelter said. He threw his saddle and roll up, stepped back and then regretted ever volunteering to ride up on top.

She stepped out of the coach with practiced grace. A young, beautiful woman with flaming red hair, dancing green eyes. She was full breasted and elegant in a green satin skirt with a ruffled white blouse. A tiny green hat perched on her hair which gleamed in the sun, becoming copper and pale gold as she moved.

Shelter removed his hat but she stepped past him without noticing him. Cold as ice. Look at that, Shell thought. Shining like fire and all iceberg underneath.

The other passengers had been rattled by an Indian attack. They looked trail-dusty and weary. But not this one. She strode across the yard as if she were crossing a ballroom, her face composed, her carriage erect, her hips swaying gently from side to side.

"Ten dollars," Windy said wryly.

"What's that?"

"I figured you'd want to set inside now. But you're wastin' your time. I seen that type before."

Shell smiled. "Yeah, I guess I have too. What a waste though, Windy. My God, what a waste."

Shelter reached up, gripped the bar and stepped into the box. Sweat was trickling down his cheek and his shirt was stuck to his chest. The sun was low but it hadn't cooled off any.

"This is the tough part of the trip," Windy said. "Sun right in my eyes—cain't see a damned thing."

"You carrying trouble?" Shelter asked, glancing at the strong box under Windy's seat.

"Enough," the driver answered warily. His expression changed suddenly. "Here she comes, the lady barrister."

Shelter followed the driver's eyes. The redhead was stepping from the porch of the station, hoisting her skirts daintily as she walked toward the stage. The blonde and her escort remained on the porch, but Windy waved them on.

"I'm pullin' out in two minutes!"

"Barrister, did you say?" Shelter asked with disbelief. The redhead walked coolly past their stares and climbed into the coach. They could feel the stage shift as she settled down.

"Somethin', ain't it," Windy commented. "But that's what I hear. She's a fee-male lawyer, my friend. Goin' West to try for a start—back East they laughed her out of court, or so they say."

"Wait until she sees what a courtroom out here can turn into," Shell said thoughtfully. A case was liable to be tried in a saloon with the judge pounding his gavel on a beer barrel and the jury catcalling the defendant, the gallery shouting taunts at the lawyers: "Hang the bastard and reopen the bar!"

Well, maybe she could handle that. Tucson was becoming sophisticated now. Phoenix was citi-fied. "Where's she going to hang her shingle?"

"Crater," Windy said, and he snapped the reins, rolling out onto the broad, empty desert as the sun sagged toward the saw-toothed mountains to the west.

The coach lurched forward and swung down the road into the sandy draw where not a breath of wind stirred, where the shadows formed a brief dark river. Then, the four bays laboring, they climbed onto the desert where the sun baked the sands, where nothing at all lived but the sidewinder, the scorpion, and the Apache.

They rolled on, the coach jolting over the rough road, past an abandoned adobe where a man's dreams had crumbled away, been baked by the scorching sun or bled by war axes.

Shelter sat with his hat tugged low to shield his eyes from the fierce sun, his Winchester in hand. Here on the flats there was little to worry about, but gradually the land humped, and the hills, deep in shadow, formed hiding places. There was much greasewood now, much cholla cactus as they wound along the red hills, and here and there a few deprived cedar trees.

"The Tanner Line," Windy said above the rumble of the horses' hooves, "it's been a hard luck story. Eight stations between Fort Thomas and Tucson. Three of them are closed on and off until Ben Tanner can find another poor sucker to live out on this Apache infested, godforsaken, sun-whipped land.

"Me, I don't know why I stick. This is the driest, most bloody hunk of creation I ever seen. I never know when I'll get hit. Never know when I'll find

14

a station burned out, the station manager massacred. They've just upped and taken off from time to time—the smart ones. Sometimes they take the horses, leaving me to walk my heat-shriveled ponies home.

"Worst of all Tanner had the good fortune to land the contract for the Camby Mines in Tucson. That means we're carrying payroll half the time. Going west, that is. And it ain't no mystery to the locals. I've been hit four times Shelter. Lost two shotgun men, one over-anxious passenger, sixteen horses. They usually cut 'em loose to give themselves a good long head start," he explained.

"Anybody know who's doing it?" Shelter asked.

"Nobody that's talkin'. Folks have their ideas, though."

"They usually do," Shelter said. And most of the time they were wrong.

The sun showed only as a brilliant golden ball between the dark hills. The desert lay in shadow. The air was cooling rapidly, bringing blessed relief.

They had entered an ancient, time-eroded canyon where the shadows dominated all. The sky overhead was flame red. "Through the notch," Windy said, "and you'll be able to see Crater."

Shelter looked ahead to the pale patch of sky between two black, hulking bluffs. The wagon road ran along the dry streambed below them and up over a rocky hump. Then, Windy said, it led through the notch and out onto the flats again for the last mile into Crater.

They never reached the notch.

In a shallow dip a rotted log lay across the road. The lead horse hit it, stumbled and went down, dragging its harness mate with it. Windy, cussing and shouting, tried to pull the horses to their feet by main force, but it was already too late.

The lead bay had broken a foreleg just above the fetlock and had crumpled up. The others slammed into it, whinnying, going to their hind legs in confusion. Horseflesh collided with horseflesh and the coach tilted up crazily on two wheels.

Shelter had to hang on as the coach itself hit the log, bounced high into the air and came down astraddle the log. A wheel splintered and gave. It spun off into the ravine and the passengers were thrown violently sideways.

The blonde screamed and then screamed again as the guns opened up from out of the darkness.

2

The first shot jerked Windy to his feet and tore half his throat away. He glanced at Shelter with wide white eyes, made a small gurgling protest, and toppled forward onto the back of a panicked horse.

Shelter left the box in a long dive. He saw the stabbing tongues of flame from the concealed guns, heard the bullets chew into the stagecoach, saw the horses trampling each other in their bewilderment. Then he hit the ground hard.

The breath rushed from his lungs and his shoulder ached, but he didn't slow down to worry about that. He kept on rolling. Down the long gravelly slope he rolled, the Winchester clenched tightly in his hand.

He slammed to an abrupt, painful stop against the side of a boulder, and gasping for breath he scrambled several yards before hurling himself against the earth. He lay there panting, eyes alert, the rifle cool in his hand.

The male passenger lay sprawled half in, half out of the coach, dead. The blonde woman lay on top of him as if in trying to protect him she had taken a bullet.

Shelter crept up the grade, his eyes searching the cold shadows. He saw a dark, masked figure vault to the box and squeezed off a shot. The highwayman spun around and went down in a heap.

Shelter rolled aside. A dozen shots from above peppered the earth where he had lain moments before. How many guns? Where? He tried to organize his thoughts, to formulate a plan.

The hail of bullets destroyed his concentration. His only concern suddenly was to live. He pressed his face to the earth and listened to the roar of the guns, the deadly whine of bullets. He could hear the nasty little *whishhh* of flying particles of lead, bullets which could tear a man to chunks of bleeding meat, smash bone, and sever tendons.

Shelter lifted his head a fraction of an inch and saw another bandit stealthily moving toward the strongbox, keeping low behind the downed horses.

Let him have it and be gone—what difference did it make? He wasn't paid to protect that gold. He wasn't paid to lose his life.

Logic might have dictated that, but logic didn't take into account three dead people, good people as folks went. These men were butchers, and Shell had an abiding hatred of such. Men who kill for profit, for the hell of it—they ought to be smashed like the vile little insects they are.

He settled his rifle sights on the man's chest and squeezed off, then levered another cartridge into the chamber without moving the rifle, fired again. The bandit went down.

And the night was silent.

It was dead still. That was the word for it—dead. The two passengers lay unmoving at the door of the coach. One of the outlaws was sprawled a yard from them. Shelter was sure he had gotten one other man, dead or not he could not say. And the barrister? That bothered him. He had no wish to find that pretty thing bathed in blood, life torn from her young body. But there was no movement from within the coach.

There was no movement anywhere in the canyon, but Shelter was far from certain that he was alone in the night. Those men had placed their lives on the line to take the strongbox. They wouldn't give it up easily.

Shell shifted slightly and let his hand search the earth. He found what he wanted. He closed his fingers around a small rock, still warm from the sun. Then with a sidearm motion he flipped the rock into the brush to his right.

Nothing. There was no reaction to the sound which was little comfort to Shell. It only indicated that if there was someone there, he was a professional, a careful man not given to shooting at noises in the bush.

The canyon drew darker and Shell stiffened as he lay unmoving. Stars blinked on across the sky and in the distance a coyote lifted a complaining voice to the desert night.

Shell began to move. Cautiously, noiselessly. He crawled forward up the rocky slope, rifle cradled in his arms. One of the stage horses blew and was answered by a horse in the distance, up one of the feeder canyons.

An abandoned horse or one that was being ridden? No telling. Shelter hugged the ground at the rim of the trail. The starlight glinted in the eyes of the dead woman and he was near enough to see the fallen expression of her broad mouth.

He liked none of this. He could not be sure there were no more hold-up men around until sunrise. That meant a long uncomfortable night.

Yet there was nothing else to do but wait. To wait and hope they were more impatient than he was.

The hours passed slowly. The pale halo of light in the eastern skies announced the coming of a quarter moon. The moon peered above the ragged horizon and cast shadows which lay like a pool around the coach, the unmoving bodies.

Gravel crunched under a boot and Shelter's hands tensed. His eyes flickered that way, trying to penetrate the darkness. They were making their move. They had to. After sunup they would have no chance. A man in Shelter's position could simply pick them off.

But they didn't believe that Shelter was alive or they wouldn't have tried it even now. Maybe. Maybe greed was pushing them beyond the restraints of reason.

Shelter had noticed that it had that mad capability.

The man moved. Coming forward in a low crouch. Moonlight glinted off his belt buckle. Shelter held his fire. Was he the only man, or were there others? The hold-up man slipped to the side of the coach, momentarily shielding himself from

Shell's view. Then he clambered up, looked around, holstered his pistol and hefted the strong-box.

Still Morgan held his fire. The man in the box turned and whistled, a low, carrying tone. He was answered from the feeder canyon and Shell smiled grimly. He had them now; he had them cold.

He eased along the rim of the trail, placing each foot carefully as he moved. He went a hundred yards and then, lifting a cautious head he got to his feet and dashed across the road, outlined briefly by the silver moon now high overhead.

Inching back through the deep shadows he reached the feeder canyon where he had heard the horse. He worked his way slowly through the tangle of manzanita and sage which choked off the dry arroyo and came suddenly upon the two horses.

They turned their heads, ears pricked, eyes alert. Shelter crouched down and they went back to their unenthusiastic grazing.

Shelter hunkered down to wait, but he didn't have to wait long. He heard a scraping sound—the heavy breathing of a man carrying a load—then saw the two men silhouetted against the paler sky.

One carried the strongbox over his shoulder, the other trailed him, backing away from the road, rifle in his hands.

Shell let them come closer. The first man had reached the horses when Shell said, "Over here."

The man who had been watching the backtrail whirled and without speaking, levered three wild shots through his carbine. Shelter fired once and

21

the outlaw was slammed back, his weapon clattering free.

The bandit with the strongbox dropped it as if it were red hot, pawed at his holster, and came up firing. Two shots uncomfortably close sang through the stillness of night. Then he bolted for his horse. Shell fired once, saw the man buckle up and go down, clutching his calf.

But the bandit was a desperate man and with the strength of desperation he crawled to his horse, grabbed the stirrup and let out a yell.

The horse bucked forward and caught its stride. Shelter leaped from cover, leaving his rifle. He vaulted a stand of nopal cactus, whacked his toe painfully against an unseen rock and leaped for the horse, catching it by the bridle.

The horse reared up, spun on its hind legs and struck out in confusion with its forehooves. Shelter saw a dark form roll free, saw the bandit's gun spew fire, and he ducked, coming up with his own Colt unlimbered.

"Give it up," Shelter shouted, but there was no give-up in the man. He touched off again and Shelter answered his shot with his own.

The man leaped convulsively once and lay still, a dark lump against the darker earth. And Shelter stood over him, his chest rising and falling, sweat trickling into his eye.

He prodded the bandit with his toe, but there was no need to. He already knew the man was dead. Turning he holstered his Colt and walked back for the strongbox, retrieving his rifle on the way.

Shouldering the box he walked toward the broken coach, his heart rate suddenly accelerating. The answer to a question lay in that coach, an answer he was unwilling to learn.

He threw the strongbox into the driver's box and walked to the door of the coach.

He swung it open and found her lying motionlessly on the seat, her eyes open to the silver moonlight, her red hair in tangled profusion.

"It's you!" she gasped, and her eyes filled with life. She watched as Shelter stepped into the coach, her mouth set in an expression of puzzled disbelief.

"Are they all . . . gone."

"All gone," he assured her, sitting beside her.

"My God." She looked at the two dead passengers in miserable fascination until Shell leaned across and closed that door, blocking out death.

"Are you all right?" he asked.

"Yes . . ." She lunged forward and Shell felt her quickened breath against his cheek, felt the liquid warmth of tears, felt her arms go around him. She held on for dear life, as if she were drowning and only he could pull her from the cold, deadly waters.

She clung to him a long moment, her shoulders twitching with barely controlled sobs, her face pressed tightly against his throat, her throat making small, childish sounds. Suddenly she went rigid and sat up, her hands slowly falling away from Shell's shoulders.

"I never . . ." She looked at him, shaking her head. Slowly the eyes took on the old haughtiness and she sat upright with wooden reserve. It was preposterous—she sat there hat askew, hair tumbling free, face streaked with tears, with three dead friends within a few yards, worrying desperately about maintaining her virginal dignity.

After all she was a university graduate! She patted her hair and said, her voice stony, "You realize that the circumstances . . ."

"I realize the circumstances, Miss—" he realized he didn't even know her name. He realized that she was a magnificent creature. "I'm Shelter Morgan," he said, offering a hand which she touched briefly with her fingertips as if the hand were an adder.

"Phoebe Strawn," she said with some dignity.

His eyes still searched hers, watching the silver of moonlight on tears, watching the fluid lips which trembled slightly.

"I'll get things straightened up and then we'll see about getting on to Crater," Shelter said. He touched his hat brim and stepped down, watching relief relax her features.

A stiff one, that. But Lord, he thought, what a beauty. He let his thoughts linger on her for a minute, on the red-gold hair, the firm, young figure, the haughty tilt of her head. Then with a deep sigh, he forced his thoughts away. There was too much to do.

Shelter slid off down the bank and by moonlight he searched for the broken wheel. It had bounced a considerable distance and when he found it, lying in the bottom of a gully, it didn't look promising. The iron tire had separated and there were three spokes broken, twisting the wheel badly.

24

He carried and dragged it back up the hill. Phoebe stood watching him, wearing a light shawl now.

"Can that be fixed?" she asked.

"I don't know," Shelter admitted. "It depends on what kind of a kit Windy carried."

Windy's kit was not bad. He apparently had had no intention of being stranded on the desert. In the boot Shell found a hammer, pliers, a length of heavy wire, and spare hub nuts.

He got to work, doing a repair job a blacksmith would have been amused at, but one which he hoped would hold until Crater.

Phoebe Strawn stood watching silently the entire time. She said nothing, neither encouraging him, nor offering a hand.

"It's taking a long time," she said impatiently when Shelter was nearly done.

"It certainly is, lady," Shelter said angrily. "It could have gone a little faster but some of us didn't want to get our pretty pink hands dirty."

"I'm not a wheelwright," she said.

"No. You're a lawyer, I keep forgetting. Why didn't you learn a *useful* trade if you wanted to work?"

Her mouth fell open but she made no reply. Shell stood, wiping his hands on his jeans, surveying the wired, lopsided wheel. "Well, it might carry us into Crater. Windy said it's only a mile or so."

"I could have walked it by this time," Phoebe snapped.

"You still might," Shelter warned her. They

faced each other stiffly for a moment before Shelter realized that was getting him nowhere.

"You'll have to ride up in the box," he told her.

"Up there?" Her finger pointed that way unsteadily. "Why not inside?"

"We're going to have a load inside," Shell said, putting the tools back into the boot. "But if you really want to ride in with a load of corpses, I suppose it's all right."

"Oh . . . I didn't . . ." She saw by the moonlight that Morgan was actually grinning and it infuriated her.

"You're evil, Mr. Morgan!"

"Yes, ma'am, so some have said." He removed his hat, wiped his brow on his shirtsleeve and nodded. "We'll be ready to roll real quick now."

She had turned her back and Miss Phoebe Strawn made no reply. Shell walked to the door on the opposite side and began the unpleasant task. He lifted the blonde into the coach and placed the man beside her. The bandit went on the floor.

It was dirty work, battlefield work, and Shelter had no liking for it. But he would not leave them for the coyotes.

Walking to the front of the coach he set the brake and then rolled the dead log off the road. He cut the downed horse from the harness and then clambered into the box.

"Come on, Lady Strawn."

She turned slowly, and by the feeble light of the moon he could see the heat in her cheeks. She bit her lip and walked to the coach. "How do I get up?"

"Best way you can," he said, tilting his hat forward. "Why, ma'am! I never heard a lady lawyer say *that*."

She settled herself primly and Shelter snapped the reins, giving a yell. The coach lurched forward throwing her off balance and she shot him a poisonous glance.

"One more stop," he told her. There was no answer. He halted at the mouth of the feeder canyon, wrapped the ribbons around the brake, and climbed down. Phoebe Strawn watched him go.

He was a tall, rugged, hateful man and she was impatient for the journey to be over. It was the most ghastly episode in her life—and that man, instead of making it easier for her, insisted on making jokes or berating her. She had heard things were different in the West, that the men were as rough as any savage Indian. This one certainly was.

Shelter found the horses and the two dead bodies. He lifted the men and threw them over the saddles, lashing them wrist-to-ankle with their own belts.

He led the grim procession out of the canyon and tied the horses on behind the coach. Then, silently, he climbed back into the box, took up the reins and started the team forward.

He walked the horses up the remainder of the grade. The coach on that dilapidated wheel swayed and jolted. Finally they topped out the grade, and rolling through the notch they could make out the dark outlines of the town of Crater, lying on the moon-glossed, empty desert. Shelter let the weary horses catch their breath and then started them homeward.

They rolled up the dusty, dark main street an hour later, passing dark-eyed, false-fronted buildings. A dog arose from the center of the street and walked with the stiffness of age to the safety of the boardwalk.

The sheriff's office was dark and silent. Shell got down and banged on the door. Phoebe climbed down awkwardly and started off.

"Where are you going?" Shelter asked.

"To find a hotel."

"Don't you think the sheriff might want to talk to you?"

"It can wait until morning," she answered sharply. "Besides, there's no one here!"

But there was. A lantern went on and they could hear grumbling and the stamping of boots. A moment later the door opened and a man of middle years with the swollen expression of sleep on his sagging face peered out.

"You the sheriff?" Shelter asked. The man nodded and Shell told him, "We've got us a little problem out here."

3

It was three hours before Shelter got away from the sheriff's office. By then the office was aglitter with light, several men in underwear and robes waited on the boardwalk, peering in the window. The local doctor had been called in as a coroner and the sheriff, Frank Snowden, painstakingly copied down Shell's statement in a cramped hand, his mouth screwed up as if it took the greatest effort of concentration.

"They killed a woman. That won't go down easy around here," Snowden grumbled.

"I think that was an accident," Shelter told him, explaining the way the bodies had lain as if the woman had leaped in front of her man, attempting to shield him. "At any rate, I don't suppose it matters now. They're all dead."

"Sure of that are you?" Snowden asked, yawning.

"Pretty much. Maybe in daylight you can read their tracks up there. But I think that was all of them."

"When," Phoebe Strawn demanded, "are we

going to be finished with all of this?"

A face in the window leered at Phoebe and she gave a little shriek. Snowden rose, closed the curtain, and sat down again. Outside they could hear the undertaker and his crew working. A shrill curse rose briefly in the night air.

Snowden sat down, composed and thoughtful. "As soon as I take your statement, miss, you can leave."

"But Mr. Morgan told you . . ."

"Miss, as a lawyer, you know I've got to interview you separately." Snowden lifted a white eyebrow, appeared ready to add something else, but spat on the floor instead, to Phoebe's disgust.

"I'll be at the nearest hotel," Shelter said, rising.

"That's the Dorchester. Block down, block to the right," Snowden said.

"Good night then." Shell grinned and nodded to Phoebe Strawn. "Good night, Miss Strawn."

Phoebe puckered her lips dryly and turned a delicate shade of pink. Shelter laughed out loud, turned, and strode through the door out into the torchlit street.

"Something the matter?" Snowden asked.

Phoebe realized then that she had been sitting staring at the closed door for a long minute. "No," she said nervously smoothing her skirt. "It's just— that man, he's insufferable. Why, the way he acted on the trail!"

"Don't like him?"

"Certainly not," Phoebe shot back. Snowden nodded slowly. "He did nothing but insult me, jeer at me . . ."

"And, so it seems, miss," the sheriff said, shuffling the papers on which Shell's statement was scribbled, "he saved your life."

Phoebe sat rigidly for a moment. She hadn't thought of it in exactly those terms. Now she did and it was undoubtedly true. She glanced again toward the door and then began answering Snowden's slow, drawling questions which she did with only half of her attention. There was a crazy, distracting buzzing going on in the back of her mind, and to her complete bafflement a warm flush was spreading slowly up her neck, burning two crimson spots on her cheekbones.

"Miss?" the sheriff said again and she realized she had not been listening.

"Please," she said, slightly flustered, "go on. I'm just a little tired."

"Yes, Miss Strawn." The old man was expressionless, but his eyes twinkled infuriatingly. "Now then, when the first shot was fired . . ."

The mockingbird perched on the ledge of the window, piped a few raucous notes and fluttered away into the brilliant morning sunshine. It was already hot outside. Shelter rose, shaking his head wearily, and walked to the wash basin on the bureau. He rinsed his face and chest and walked to the window, drying himself.

The desert spread in the distance with empty grandeur. A broad reddish mesa rose abruptly from the sands, remarkably out of place. Protected by its caprock, the mesa had endured for eons while the land around it was washed away by wind and infrequent rain.

Beyond the mesa the saw-toothed mountains rose. Shelter could even make out the notch which rose above the wagon road.

Crater itself was just as desolate, but far less appealing than the desert. A sometime-creek ran along the northern boundary. There a few sycamores and a mat of willow brush grew. A lonesome adobe, apparently uninhabited, sat near the river, an early settler's bulwark against the elements and the Apaches.

The town began with a series of tilted, primitive shacks of discarded lumber, sheet metal, and canvas on the eastern perimeter. Then the Main Street began, the dozen false-fronted buildings, two of them unpainted. Two saloons, an emporium, the hotel, and a sleepy, empty building, purpose unknown.

Back from the road a few white frame houses sat. The homes of the properous merchants, the local banker, the judge if there was a judge. It looked like a hundred other towns to a man who has traveled through those hundred others, searching.

But the signs of erosion were already there. The unpainted buildings would never be painted. Sand drifted against the weather-grayed plank-walk along Main Street. The cruel sun ate away the paint and veneer of Crater. It was dying and didn't even know it.

Shelter shaved slowly, becoming aware of a hunger slowly building. He could smell, or imagined he could, bacon frying somewhere.

He dusted his gray hat, wiped back his dark hair, and buttoned his shirt. Planting the hat squarely on his head he went out into the corridor and down the uncarpeted stairs to the lobby.

"Morning," Shelter said to the night clerk who waited with pouched, red eyes for his relief. "Where can I get some breakfast?"

A lazy, ink-stained finger lifted toward a door across the lobby and Shelter walked that way, his boot heels clicking on the plank floor.

He opened the door and was met by a rush of sound and smells. The room was thirty feet long by twenty feet wide. Two long plank tables ran the length of the room and some rough men of assorted professions sat to them, eating lustily. A cowboy, a few teamsters, a storekeeper already in his apron.

There were a few smaller tables set to one side where travelers and hotel guests ate with more decorum. Shelter seated himself at the plank table among the flying elbows and furiously clacking silverware. He didn't want solitude just then; he had questions to ask.

The huge, half-breed waitress took his order silently and vanished.

Shelter found himself sitting between two men: a cowboy, who wore old cavalry trousers and a spanking new Smith & Wesson in a battered holster, and a sullen, long-jawed teamster. Across from him a white-haired, dirty prospector shoveled potatoes and eggs into his mouth with deliberate enthusiasm.

"Wondered if someone could help me," Shelter

said. "I'm looking for my cousin."

"What's his name?" the prospector asked without pausing. His mouth was crammed full of spuds and eggs and his words were barely decipherable.

"Well, that's the thing," Shelter said, tipping his hat back. "Used to be Amos Morgan. But old Amos, he had some trouble back home. A man was killed."

The cowboy's eyes flickered toward Shell. Shell grinned, moving his elbow as the waitress placed a steaming platter in front of him. Eggs, potatoes, steak, and bisuits with honey.

"He's on the run is he?" the cowboy asked as Shelter began eating.

"He was, but he don't need to be now. A man was killed as I said and they blamed Amos. He came West to save his neck. Thing is, Verlon Hyatt—he's our neighbor, a mile south—said his conscience got to him and he couldn't take living with murder on his soul. He come forward and confessed."

"Cleared your cousin?"

"Did, for a fact. Thing is, Amos couldn't know about that away out here. He's got a wife and five kids back in Tennessee. Family sent me out to fetch him."

"Mebbe he's got a new family out here by now," the prospector commented.

"It's a possibility, isn't it?" Shelter responded with a smile. "Then that would be up to Amos. The thing is, a man has the right to know. Must be

34

touch sleeping in the shadow of that hangman's noose."

Everyone agreed that it would be. The cowboy asked, "What's your cousin look like?"

Carefully then Shelter described Du Rose in as much detail as possible, keeping his expression innocent and friendly. He thought he saw awareness flicker in the eyes of the cowhand, but he could not be sure.

"Sounds like Marcy Trammel," the teamster said, speaking for the first time.

"Marcy Trammel's dead, Henry," the prospector said.

"I know he's dead! Still could be the man."

"That would be a shame," the cowboy said thoughtfully. He had begun rolling a smoke. "Find him out you was too late."

"It would be indeed," Shelter agreed, finishing his biscuits, pouring himself a second cup of coffee from the communal pot.

Nothing would have pleased him more than to find Du Rose dead, however. It would be anticlimactic in a way, but it would have saved much effort.

The prospector, no doubt, remembered, "Marcy Trammel was a Texas boy. And no doubt about that the way he talked, his rig, way he bragged about the blasted state."

"You're right," the cowboy agreed. "From down around San Antonio. He knows all the cattle trails . . . he knew them all."

"What happened to Trammel?" Shelter asked.

"Marcy thought two pair beat a full house," the prospector said without a trace of a smile. "The other fellow begged to differ."

Shelter finished his breakfast. The conversation had drifted to a discussion of whether Marcy Trammel, if alive could have outshot Percy Freegate, also deceased.

Outside it was nearly a hundred degrees although it was not yet ten o'clock. The town sagged, looking parched and very dirty. A single horseman rode up the main street of Crater, his horse dragging its hooves, sending up tiny plumes of dust with each lazy step.

Shelter moved down the street slowly, his eyes searching each face. It would be difficult to find Du Rose. The man would have a much easier time locating Shelter.

He walked into the mercantile store, a small bell tinkling over the door. A man with a pencil behind his ear looked up expectantly.

Shell was too early. There was no one shopping yet save a single old woman.

The saloons were doing a thriving business at the time. But ordering a beer, starting an idle conversation with the bartender, he learned nothing, saw no one who resembled Du Rose.

By supper time Shell had scoured the town itself pretty well. There was no sign of Du Rose or of Sam Rutledge. Sam had scribbled that letter and then vanished.

Du Rose here.

Dammit, Sam! Where? Where in hell is he? Shelter wondered.

He splurged and bought himself a bath at the barber's shop, engaging the man in a long conversation.

"Rutledge? Short man with a Georgia accent?"

"That's the one."

The barber stopped massaging his own scalp with rose water long enough to turn and fix a fierce scowl on Morgan who was soaking in the wooden tub, eyes half-closed.

"He a friend of yours?"

"I'm not paying any of his bills," Shelter answered with a smile. The barber laughed.

"If you were, you'd have a deal of paying to do. Sure, I recall him. He was playing cards when he came to Crater. I don't think he did well at that. After maybe a month or so he came in here and asked for the works. Shave, bath, tonic. He had him a new suit and hat. And a sample case."

"Sample case?"

"That's right. He was selling patent medicine. Had some vita-tonic, as he called it, and some sort of stuff that was supposed to restore your hair. Well, I guess he did all right with that for a time. Traveled all over the county. Rutledge has a good line of patter."

"That he does," Shell agreed. He stepped from the tub, toweling off as the barber watched thoughtfully. So Sam had done some traveling in this area, had he. If he saw Du Rose it could have been anywhere within a hundred miles of Crater itself. More hard luck.

"So Rutledge drifted on, did he?"

"If you can call getting thrown on the afternoon

coach and horsewhipped drifting on."

"What happened?" Shelter sat in a chair and stamped his boots on.

"That hair restorer. Old Mrs. Gunnison thought her hair was getting a little thin on the crown and she bought some of that stuff from Rutledge. Turned her hair orange and it started falling out in big chunks. What a sight, and was her old man mad. Jesus!

"They flushed Rutledge from his hotel room and ran him right on out of town that morning."

Well, that explained the hastily scrawled letter anyway. Rutledge hadn't had much time. He smiled and shook his head conjuring up an image of Sam standing before the orange-headed woman and her furious husband. That was one scrape he hadn't been able to talk himself out of, silver tongue or no.

"Thanks," Shelter said, paying the barber. As he did so it was with the sinking realization that he was down to his last two dollars and had need of a horse. He intended to see some country.

Shelter stood on the boardwalk, grateful for the evening's deepening shadows. *Where?* Du Rose was out there somewhere, but Sam had covered a deal of country. He walked slowly back toward the hotel. He heard the tinkling of an out-of-tune piano from the saloon, and glancing up he saw the newly painted shingle hanging before the building across the street.

Shelter crossed the street behind a hay wagon and ducked under the hitch rail, stepping onto the walk. A lantern burned low within the shop. The door was open and Shelter could hear the soft humming.

The woman wore an apron and was vigorously applying the broom to the floor. Her flaming red hair was knotted at the base of her neck.

"How about supper?"

Phoebe spun, startled at the sudden sound. Her eyes narrowed as she spied the long, dark man leaning against the wall, arms folded on his chest.

"Well . . . you startled me. What did you say?"

"I said, how about some supper? It's nearly time."

"No thank you, Mr. Morgan."

"Just like that?" he asked.

"I don't think it's—"

"I'm not fit company?"

"It's not that," she said irritably.

"All right. How's everything going here?"

"Fine," she said with evident relief. "I met a man who let me have this office for practically nothing." She looked around her. "I think it will do."

"You've got to watch these generous offers from men, Miss Strawn. The man may have other motives."

"Really!" she said in exasperation. "Just because Mr. Quail . . ."

Shelter stepped nearer to her. So near that her breasts nearly touched his chest. He stood towering over her, looking down with those icy blue eyes which caused her flesh to break out in goosebumps.

She went on bravely, "After all, just because a

man makes an offer of friendship . . ." she laughed, not effectively. She could feel the heat of his body. Her pulse quickened. "Just because you offered to take me to supper, for instance, I certainly didn't think you had any devious motive."

"You didn't?"

"Of course not." Her eyes shuttled away. Shelter caught the soft fragrance of her. He watched the lanternlight gleam in her sleek hair.

"Well, that's my point," he grinned. "You never do know. I know I certainly had other motives than friendliness."

"I should hope so."

"You're an outstanding woman, Miss Strawn. Polished, smart, and above all, very beautiful, very intriguing . . . physically."

"Mr. Morgan!" She backed away a step and there was outrage in her eyes. But beyond that outrage was some other emotion. Some spark of interest, some awareness of her own.

"What is this? What's happening here!"

Shelter turned to see the bulky, yellow-haired man in the doorway. He wore a gray town suit and his fists were clenched.

"Bert!"

Bert Quail came into the shop, looking from Phoebe to Shelter and back again. "Who is this man?"

"Bert, this is Mr. Morgan, the man from the stage."

"Oh that one," Quail said in a way which indicated Phoebe had discussed Morgan with him, and that it had not been a flattering discussion.

40

"Mr. Morgan, Mr. Quail."

Shell nodded. Quail kept on coming. He was a big man, broad-shouldered and probably thought of himself as hard. But beneath his flesh Shelter could see the town softness of his muscles, the toughness of a man who has never been tested, because of his imposing size, never had his self-image shattered. He kept on coming.

"Is he bothering you, Phoebe? What did he want?"

At that Phoebe Strawn blushed furiously. It was not helpful.

Quail's eyes narrowed. "I think you had better get out of here, Mr. Morgan."

"I was just leaving," Shell said amiably. "If you won't consent to have supper with me, Miss Strawn . . ."

"Now," Quail said, and then he made his mistake. He stepped to Shelter, grabbed his shoulder and spun him around.

Quail was trembling, his face red. Shelter heard Phoebe give a little squeal. "Take that hand off me," Shelter said. His voice was mild, but there was a definite warning in it.

Bert Quail wasn't perceptive enough to read the warning. He was a big, rough-mannered man and used to riding roughshod over people.

"And if I don't?" Quail sneered. Shelter didn't let him finish the question.

Shell's left arm came up and slapped Quail's hand away before the big man could react. Then Shelter stunned him with a right hook which traveled no more than a foot but had all of his power behind it. Quail, to give him his due, didn't go down, and Shelter grunted his astonishment.

Quail was dirty enough, but he was no fighter. He made do with what he had. He picked up a straight-backed wooden chair and with a scream of fury arced it through the air, trying to crush Shelter's skull.

Shell saw it coming and had time to get his arm up, ducking at the same time. The chair smashed into his arm, and for a moment Shell thought it had been broken. His shoulder was shot full of pain, his lower arm numb.

Quail, sensing the kill, moved in. But Morgan had tangled with more than one would-be bad man. He feinted left, kicked out hard with a boot which caught Quail a glancing blow just below the kneecap, and then with his right he drove upward, catching Bert in the wind.

The big man staggered back, doubled up at the waist, holding his soft gut. Shell waded in, swinging away one-armed. He chopped down on Quail's jaw, spinning his head around and then came up, catching him on the point of the chin.

Quail's teeth clacked together and his head was jolted back. Blood spurted from his mouth. Quail put up his hands in a childlike gesture and Shell finished him.

Quail never saw the right hand coming. He was trying to blink away the lights, the bluish haze which had settled in behind his eyes. The right caught him flush on the jaw and he went down hard, folding up and lying motionlessly on the floor.

A few drops of blood leaked from Quail's nose, staining the newly swept floor. He slept peacefully for now. When he came around he would have a mountain-sized headache.

Shelter staggered back, testing his arm which seemed to be okay now as the sensation flooded back into it. He bent, picked up his hat and turned to face Phoebe Strawn.

"Miss Strawn, I'm sorry."

She screamed, cutting off his apology. She was pale. She clutched her apron at the throat, twisting it. Her eyes were wild with accusation.

"You're a savage! A savage!"

"Phoebe." He stepped toward her, smiling, but she backed away like a cornered animal, not stopping until her back was pressed against the wall.

"Get out of here." Her voice was cracked, dry. "Go on, now."

"All right. Does that mean we won't be having supper?" He couldn't resist asking, but he knew she was in no mood for it.

She watched him warily, as if he might turn on her next. She seemed not to recall that Quail had started it. He shrugged, touched his hat brim, and walked toward the door feeling wronged.

Looking back from the street he could see Phoebe Strawn kneeling beside Quail, cradling his hand, and Shelter ground his teeth together. It was enough to make a man swear off women altogether—well, almost.

He walked back to his hotel room, stripped off his torn shirt and washed up. Then, counting his change, he went down to supper. There was enough for that one last meal and one more night in the hotel.

After that he would be broke. Broke and no closer to finding Du Rose than ever. Not only that—he had made a strong enemy in Bert Quail. He didn't know how strong until the sheriff came thumping on his hotel room door.

4

Frank Snowden stood in the dimly lit, musty corridor, looking sober and competent. The star on his vest glinted in the lantern light which fell through Shell's doorway.

"Forget something?" Shelter asked.

"Nope. It's not about the hold-up," the sheriff answered.

"No?" Shell cocked his head curiously. "Come on in."

Snowden did, his piercing gray eyes automatically making an inspection of the sparsely furnished room.

"Sit down," Shell invited.

"All right. Thanks," Snowden said with a nod. His mouth beneath his brushed white mustache was drawn into a straight, expressionless line.

"Well," Shelter asked amiably, "what is it?"

"It's trouble, is what it is," Snowden said without malice.

"I don't get you." Shelter sat on the end of the bed watching the lawman's eyes.

"Half an hour ago I got a complaint about you

from Bert Quail." The sheriff lifted an eyebrow. "I believe you've met him."

"Briefly."

"With him was Miss Phoebe Strawn who witnessed an attack you made on Quail."

"An attack!" Shelter laughed and Snowden lifted a hand.

"Wait a minute. You hit the man, didn't you?"

"Yes, but—"

"All right. Let me give you the rest of it." Snowden crossed his legs and hung his hat on his knee. "It seems Miss Strawn has been doing some thinking about her statement. She's not all that sure that things happened the way she reported them."

"What's that supposed to mean?" Shelter wanted to know.

"She says she's not sure it was necessary for you to kill all those men. Says for all she knows you could have killed them in cold blood."

"Oh for Christ's sake," Shelter mumbled.

"Yeah." Snowden cleared his throat.

"Well? What do you think, Sheriff?"

"I had a look at those bodies, Morgan. None of them was shot in the back. And I don't think a normal man sets out to murder a gang of robbers he happens upon."

"Then what's the problem?"

"The problem is she's hot about it. More importantly, Bert Quail's hot about it. I'd say he steered her into her present line of thinking."

"Who is Quail?"

"That is a different subject." Snowden thought

46

it over for a minute. "He is a big man, Morgan. At least in Crater. His father founded this town. Bert inherited the old man's power if not his wisdom."

"So when he speaks, you jump."

Snowden didn't like that a bit. His jaw clenched. "No. If I did, you'd be locked up right now, Morgan. The thing is, the man has wealth and political power. He wants you locked up or out of town. It's not all that bad an idea," Snowden said frankly. The lantern light hardened the lines of his face.

"Tell me, Morgan, just what are you doing here? You've been all over town asking questions."

Shelter repeated the story of the cousin which sounded lame even to him. The sheriff wasn't buying it, that was obvious. But without knowing what was what in this town he wasn't about to name Du Rose. Du Rose could be another local with "wealth and political power."

"I don't like that," the sheriff said, shaking his head. "I don't like that." He might have been speaking to himself. Snowden stood abruptly. "I think maybe it's time for you to travel on, Morgan—unless you've some lawful employment or other solid reason for hanging around Crater. If there was a Cousin Amos, he ain't here, I'll guarantee you that. Someone's pulling your leg."

Someone was, that was certain. He tried to read Snowden's character and failed. The man had spent a lifetime wearing a mask and a badge.

"All right," Shell agreed, apparently to Snowden's surprise. Those white eyebrows were hoisted again. There was no point in telling the lawman he was planning on pulling out anyway.

Where he would be going he could not have said, nor could he have said how. He had no horse and no money in his pockets. He had been thinking about washing dishes or shoveling out stables for long enough to buy a horse. That was now out of the question.

He would be leaving town afoot, walking into the Apache-infested desert. Thanks to Bert Quail and the beautiful and so changeable Miss Phoebe Strawn.

The sheriff bade him goodnight as if they were parting friends, but his gray eyes were not friendly.

Closing the door Shelter sagged onto the bed, his hands behind his head, staring at the stained ceiling.

Du Rose here.

He dozed off and had a brief bloody memory of Jeb Thornton spilling from his horse, his face shot away, his mouth open in a soundless scream, of Du Rose laughing . . . the tap at the door brought him out of it.

Rubbing his eyes Shelter crossed the room. The lantern had burned out and he did not relight it. He carried his revolver beside his thigh.

"Who is it?"

"Shelter Morgan?"

"That's right."

"Open up. I got a business proposition for you."

The man who stepped through the door was

shriveled and gnarled, of small stature, dried by fierce winds and tempered by the hot sun. He could have been any age. He thrust out a hickory hand to Shell and removed a battered, dusty hat.

"Yeah, you look like I conjured," he said, squinting at Morgan. He saw the Colt and chuckled with delight. "Put the light on, boy. I ain't no Guthrie."

"What's a Guthrie?" Shell asked, shoving the Colt behind his belt then lifting the lantern chimney to light it. The old man chuckled again.

"You ought to know. You killed four, five of 'em."

"The outlaws?"

"The same. Mind if I set?" Without waiting for an answer he did set. "I'm Willie Tanner, Morgan." At Shell's blank expression, he added, "Tanner Line Stagecoach Company. You rode shotgun for me, although I don't recall hiring you."

"You own the stage line."

"Such as it is. Patched and wired together, plagued by them infernal Apaches and the Guthrie boys. Such as it is, I own it. How 'bout working for me?" he asked, squinting at Shell.

"All right." Shelter didn't even hesitate. What better way of seeing the county, of talking to people. Besides, there was a single dime in Shell's pocket and he had been warned out of Crater.

"Thought you'd argue a bit," Willie Tanner said. "You know what kind of problem I've got. Are you that hard-up or that crazy?"

"A little of both," Shelter said with a grin. "I

was ready to move on anyway."

Willie laughed again, a dry secretive cackle. "So I was given to understand, Mr. Morgan, so I understood."

They rode out together at sunrise, backs to the rising sun. A flourish of color overwhelmed the desert. Red sands streaked with deep purple met the blue-violet of the rising, barren hills. A jackrabbit loped lazily away from their approaching horses. Long crooked shadows lay beneath the mammoth saguaro cactus. Along the sandy wash mesquite grew and Shelter saw the tracks of a peccary tribe.

"It's alive," Willie Tanner said in response to some unspoken comment. "Folks think there's nothin' livin' out here, but they ain't got the eyes to see. How the hell do they think the Apache lives out here? There's water for those sharp enough to find it. Wild boar, jackrabbits, up in them hills," his chin lifted, "desert sheep and mule deer. Underfoot there's food to eat, but many a starvin' man has missed it.

"She's a beautiful, lonesome place, this desert, but it's a stern land, almighty stern with the unwary. Do you know desert ways?"

"Not well," Shelter admitted. "I've ridden it some, eaten my share of chuckawalla and mesquite beans when I had to. That was a little farther south."

"Got tangled up in something, did you?"

"Tangled up," Shelter admitted. His thoughts strayed briefly to that long ago desert trek with the dark-eyed Drusilla.

"We'll crest this range of hills," Willie said, jabbing a finger at the cactus-studded humps which barely deserved to be called hills. "Then we're within a mile of Adobe Falls. That's my home station just now."

"Why out here?" Shelter wanted to know.

"Well," Willie answered, removing his hat to wipe his brow. "I did operate out of Crater. Figured I was a big business man, you see, out of that building where the lady lawyer's settin' up, you know the one?"

Shelter nodded. Willie's expression was humorous.

"But Corson—he was my man at Adobe Falls—got himself shot up by some night riders. It was either them darned Guthrie boys or some relatives of a Mexican gal Corson was courting on the side—either way, Corson got himself dead and I've had the devil's own time trying to replace him."

"I understand you've had the same trouble elsewhere."

"All down the line," Tanner agreed. "From Fort Thomas to Tucson. Apaches, Guthries, who-knows-who. Burned stations, burned coaches. Dead drivers, dead horses."

"All because of that gold you carry?"

"Well, a man might think so," Willie Tanner said. His eyes squinted at Shelter. The old man was tough as leather and just then his eyes showed that toughness. "But I wonder, Mr. Morgan. I surely do. The Apaches now, that can't be helped. They're after horses, guns, whatever they can find. But they're here one day, gone the next, you know.

Sooner or later the army will round them up or drive them down into Mexico again. I can suffer the Apaches.''

"But not the Guthries? It seems like they're pretty well cleaned out now, doesn't it?"

"No." Tanner shook his head. They had dipped into a sandy ravine where chocolate-colored rocks in rough tiers rose to the sky. Silver-green willow brush lined the dry watercourse.

Tanner explained. "I had a look at those bodies, Morgan. I was hopeful, but it wasn't to be. The old man, Jeremiah Guthrie and his oldest son, Caleb, they wasn't there. Just cousin Harry, the youngest son, Ike, and two nameless faces. The old man's still alive, and he'll be in a red fury. You've killed his son, Morgan, and I guess he'll be looking for you."

They came out of the arroyo and Shelter saw a long adobe and log house backed up against the base of a rising, stony bluff. Several huge sycamores surrounded the stage station.

Three coaches sat in a row to one side of the building, and three dozen horses grazed in a pole corral to the east where sparse bunch grass grew from the sandy earth.

"Adobe Falls," Tanner announced. "Let's go on down and make acquaintances."

Willie Tanner was a man for organization, despite his disheveled personal appearance. The Adobe Falls station had a place for everything, and everything seemed to be in its place.

There was no pile of trash as was common on many a ranch and way station, no fallen-down fencing. There was a blacksmith's shop beneath the trees, smoke rising from an iron chimney. A smaller outbuilding, probably a drivers' bunkhouse, sat behind the house, up the broad grassy valley where the stream flowed down onto the desert to vanish.

The lay-out was orderly. Glancing up as they emerged from the arroyo, Shelter saw another indication of Tanner's organization. Sunlight glinted on metal and Tanner lifted a hand to the rifleman who was perched on the bluff, watching the approach to Adobe Falls.

"Haven't never had an attack on Adobe Falls," Tanne winked, "but it don't hurt to take out a little insurance."

"Is that the only guard," Shelter asked, "or are there others?"

Tanner looked at him oddly. Shelter was studying the landforms and the lay-out of the buildings in a way which reminded him of something.

"You a military man, Morgan?"

"I was," Shell answered.

"Seen it in your eyes. You see things different. Look at the defenses, see the terrain as a battlefield."

"It's automatic," Shell shrugged.

"It's damned useful out here," Tanner said. With satisfaction he added, "I knew I picked the right man."

They tied up at the hitch rail which had a watering trough beneath it for the horses. Shelter loosened his cinches, slipped his horse's bit and followed Tanner onto a swaying wooden porch.

"Come along inside," Tanner offered and Shell, dusting himself off, removing his hat, went in.

The smell of coffee was rich, the lingering scent of lye soap faint. The floors were wooden and had been recently scrubbed. The heat of the day hadn't dried them as yet.

"I brought a new man," Willie Tanner said, and in response Shelter heard a pan crash down in a concealed kitchen. He waited expectantly as bootheels clicked across the plank floor and then she appeared, holding a dishtowel in her hands.

"How long will this one last," she said snappishly.

Shelter lifted his eyes to her and smiled. A young woman, no more than five feet tall with long dark hair, stood drying her hands on the dishtowel, a sharp gleam in her dark eyes, a nearly impish expression on her pursed lips.

She wore a man's flannel shirt which hardly concealed the enthusiastic thrust of her full breasts. Her hips threatened to split the seams of a worn pair of jeans. She caught Shelter's appraising eyes sweeping over her figure, and she placed a hand on her hip, rolled her eyes and sighed.

"Not another one of *those*."

"I don't reckon they can help it, Ellie," Tanner said. "This is my niece, Ellie Tanner, Mr. Morgan. Forgive her saucy ways, I guess my upbringing ain't been quite right."

"That's all right," Morgan said. He was getting used to hostile women. But Ellie's hostility wasn't genuine, and he knew it. It was mock anger, frustration with the male race, probably adopted to keep the boys at arms' length in this isolated station.

"I reckon we could use some grub, Ellie, if you don't mind," Tanner suggested.

"Set," she said and they did, Tanner grinning as she walked away, shoulders set.

"She's a hell of a girl," Tanner said with evident pride. "She can ride, shoot, set you to laughing . . . her folks, my brother and his wife, Bess, they ran Dog Creek Station—you'll see where that is—but the Guthries burned it down and killed 'em. Folks thought it was the Apaches, but I know Apache work when I see it. It wasn't no Indian raid."

Tanner's voice lowered. "Found the little gal, she was eight years old, found her curled up in the wood bin outside the corral, big nasty-looking Colt Walker in her tiny hands. And I don't doubt for a minute that she'd of used it had I been someone else." His voice raised jovially, "Nothin' like a good breakfast," he said as Ellie returned with two platters.

"Yeah," she said with the mock sourness which was a portion of her stock in trade and, as Shelter already recognized, was not meant to be taken seriously, "Nothing like a nice breakfast even if it's already nearly noon and you're not the one who has to cook it."

Tanner grinned and Shell suppressed a smile. Obviously the food had been kept warm just for the old man. Ellie stood, hands on hips, one hip thrust out and looking Shelter over she asked,

55

"What are you, a gunhand or something?"

"Ellie!"

"Well, look at him."

"I'm not a gunhand," Shelter told her quietly, "but I'm willing to fight if I need to."

"Well," Ellie said, running her fingers through her dark jumble of hair, "that's something, I suppose. Half the men we've hired on around here get spooked at shadows and take off before they've unrolled their beds."

She looked Shelter over again, cool amusement in her eyes, "Still—you've got a certain cut about you, Mr. Morgan, and I don't know if I care for it."

With that she sauntered away, her ample, tight buttocks rolling beneath the fabric of her patched jeans. Tanner's expression was both amused and questioning. Shelter shook his head.

"Let's eat," he said, and they did.

After eating they went out into the dry heat of the desert day and Tanner walked Shell around the station. A sullen, red-faced man in leather chaps sat mending a bridle in the harness shed and Shell was introduced.

"Shelter, this is Mel Giles. He's the next driver out, so I reckon you'll be riding with him on the eastbound."

Giles nodded and Shelter returned the gesture. He had taken an instant dislike to the man, but for what reason he could not have said. Giles had yellowish eyes, bloodshot just now, a small, nearly pointed head, and an evasive smile.

"How long's he been with you?" Shelter asked as they left the harness shed.

56

"Mel?" Turner asked with surprise. "Years. He's been through hell with us, but he sticks."

The second Tanner Line driver Shell met was a wiry, glossy-haired young Mexican named Fernando Reyes. He liked this man at first sight. He had an olive complexion, black eyes, a brilliant smile, and a small, neat mustache. He had a driver's hands and the cocky confidence of the young.

"New man, eh?" Reyes said, examining Shelter. "Driver, shotgun, or station manager?"

"Whatever the boss says," Shell answered congenially.

"I think shotgun," Reyes commented with a nod. "I think you ride with Fernando to keep the Apache off my back, eh, Mr. Tanner?"

"We'll see, Fernando. First of all Morgan's got to learn the area. Then I'll decide."

"You give him to me," Fernando said, still smiling. "I know a tough hombre when I see one, and I see one now. You give him to me and we'll get through every time."

"Fernando likes you," Tanner said as they walked back toward the house.

"And Mel Giles?"

Tanner shrugged. "Mel is tired, damned tired. When a man risks his life every time he climbs into the box, after a while he gets awfully damned tired of his job."

"But Mel sticks."

"Sure. He's damned loyal."

They stopped in the shade of a sycamore. The pencil thin creek trickled past, glittering silver in the sharp sunlight. "Have you ever thought . . ." Shelter began, but Tanner interrupted him.

"That there's someone inside Tanner tipping Guthrie? Sure I've thought of it," Willie said. "But if there is, it's not Mel Giles."

"Just thinking out loud."

"You didn't like him, did you? Maybe that's what brings that suspicion to mind. Thing is, Morgan, I can't go around mistrusting the few men I do have left. I think it would drive me crazy. The only Tanner men I could trust would be those who got themselves killed."

"And maybe not them," Shell said dryly. Tanner laughed, but it was a brief, harsh laugh.

In the afternoon Tanner and Shell sat at the rough puncheon table in the station kitchen, going over maps and discussing routes. Ellie hovered about the room, doing, Shell noticed, meaningless jobs. Shelter himself felt distracted. Was any of this getting him closer to Du Rose?

He had one purpose for being in Arizona, and it was not to ride shotgun for the Tanner Line. He felt like an impostor. Tanner was outgoing, trusting.

Ellie had noticed it. At sundown as Shelter sat on the glide swing on the back porch, watching the sky go orange and deep purple, watching the raw mountains above them soften into shadow, she came and sat beside him.

He glanced at her, but she too was staring into the distance, luxuriating in the cooling breeze which flowed down the flanks of the mountains.

"What is it, Morgan?" she said finally. "Just

what is it with you?"

"I don't think I know what you're talking about," Shelter replied. A single torn cloud caught a crimson ray of light and hovered above the mountains like a flaming beacon. The slopes of the hills were a soft purple.

"What I'm talking about . . ." Ellie scooted closer to him, tucking her legs up under her; her dark eyes were intent. "I wonder what you are and who you are. I watched you with Uncle Willie. The way you listened and nodded, your eyes distracted."

"It was you distracting them," Morgan said lightly.

"No," she said soberly. "And don't grin like that. It wasn't me. Your thoughts were far away."

"Maybe. Does it matter?"

"Of course it matters! Listen, Morgan, we've had a few men through here. Some of them are just looking for a free meal and a place to sleep. When Uncle Willie needs them, they're gone."

"And you wonder if I'm one of them."

"That's right." She nodded. "Are you here to help Tanner or to help yourself to whatever you can find?"

"While I'm drawing Tanner pay I'm here to help Tanner."

"That's not an answer."

The shadows were deeper and she was nearer. He could taste the soft fragrance of her hair. His hand slipped behind her neck and she did not draw away. Her eyes were wide, her lips slightly parted, and he drew her nearer, kissing her softly, feeling

59

her breasts against him.

Her response was electric, hungry. She smothered his mouth with her own. Her hand dropped and gripped his thigh just above the knee as she pressed against him.

Abruptly she pulled away. Her laugh was short, astonished. "That's not what I came out here for at all."

"No?" Shelter looked at her intently until he saw her smile and nod her head ever so slightly.

"Maybe so. Maybe it was," she admitted. She stood then, her hand slowly sliding from his leg. "Well, I didn't learn anything, did I?"

Shell looked at her again and he grinned and she smiled in return. "Right again," Ellie said. "Maybe I did learn something."

Then she turned and was gone, and as the screen door banged shut Shelter heard her give a short, self-mocking laugh.

"All done now?" Willie Tanner asked.

Shell glanced toward the shadows and the old man came forward, his eyes twinkling.

"It looks like it," Shelter replied.

"I wasn't snooping," Willie said. He tipped back his hat and leaned his back against the porch rail. "I came to tell you that you're going out tonight. I want you to ride to Fort Thomas with Mel. Are you up to it?"

"I am."

"Good. It's eastbound to Thomas, of course, so there shouldn't be any Guthrie trouble. Who can say about the Apaches?"

"But coming back?" Shelter asked.

"Gold for the Tucson payrolls," Tanner said with a small shrug.

Then they could expect trouble. Shelter began to wonder what kind of a fool he had been to get involved in this. He had wanted only a horse, a chance to search out Du Rose. Now he was embroiled in a small war.

The Apaches would take his scalp if they had the chance, and from what Tanner had told him of Jeremiah Guthrie, even that might be preferable to what the old man would do to the man who had killed his son.

"I thought the payroll was on the last stage," Shelter said, and Tanner nodded.

"So it was, but I've written to the mine owner in Tucson and he agrees with me. The only way to stop this business is to stagger the deliveries. We can't have a fixed schedule. So we'll take next month's payroll through to Tucson now and they can hold it in the Camby Mine's office there. They've got a decent safe and plenty of armed men to watch it."

"And if we don't get through?" Shelter asked.

Tanner was silent, the darkness cloaking him. Finally he said, "If we can't deliver, Morgan, we'll go out of business sure. I need that Camby Mine contract bad. Already our passenger trade has fallen off to nil. Everyone knows that Tanner is getting hit by outlaws and Apaches. If we don't get that shipment through . . ." He shrugged. "Well, I guess you'll be looking for a new job and so will I."

5

It was almost midnight when they rolled out of Adobe Falls Station. The frosted stars glittered overhead, the desert was flat and black ahead of them. Mel Giles sat with a hunched back and a determined face beside Shelter, whipping the horses out along the wagon trail.

Shell sat beside him, shivering. The night, after the intense heat of day, was very cold.

He had nothing to warm him but the small remembrance of Ellie Tanner watching him from behind the curtain as they stepped into the box, the horses stamping, steaming from the nostrils.

He saw her dark eyes ablaze, saw the faint smile on her lips, and found it warming, a light in the cold night. But then she was gone, the horses lurching ahead, straining at the harnesses for a minute before the stage gathered momentum and dipped down through the sycamores and out onto the desert, leaving the tiny twinkling lights in the Adobe Falls house far behind.

Giles was intent on the road and the reins, but it was obvious that the horses knew the way, that

Giles knew the animals and the trail well enough to drive blindfolded.

Shelter had a Winchester propped up between his knees, a ten-gauge express gun at his feet, on the hooks fastened to the box.

The trail was rough, but it was peaceful out here. There would be no Apaches, no outlaw trouble, or shouldn't be, but Shell didn't let it lull him into a false sense of security.

That was the way men died.

He started a desultory conversation with the taciturn Mel Giles, gradually bringing him around to his main point of interest.

"You know, I've got a cousin out here somewhere," Shelter said, and he repeated the well-worn story about Cousin Amos and the law.

"Nobody like that around here," Giles said after Shelter gave him Du Rose's description.

"Well, he's out here somewhere. I had a letter from him," Shell disagreed.

"No one like that," Giles said, standing up briefly to look for a depression in the road ahead.

Shell looked at the driver silhouetted against the low stars. He was damned sure, wasn't he? Everyone else had tried to be helpful, bringing up dead men and possible look-alikes, but Giles—*he* was certain. The only one who had been.

Well, not the only one, Shell realized thinking back. Sheriff Snowden had been damned sure too. "If there was a Cousin Amos, he ain't here," Snowden had said. So what could you make of that?

Shelter tried Giles again after a few miles. "You

know, I'm certain my cousin is around here. Seems like you must have run into him somewhere."

"I never saw your cousin," Giles said irritably.

"He's a tall man, narrow-faced, long dark hair—"

"You already gave me the description!" Giles muttered to himself, whipped the horses unnecessarily, and stared intently at the desert now lighted dimly by the rising moon.

"I just thought . . ."

"I don't know him!" Giles said, and there was a fury in his voice. Enough fury to make Shell believe almost with certainty that Mel Giles did know just who he was talking about. Knew him and feared him.

Shell settled back. They reached the first stage stop an hour later. A mild woman in her forties gave them coffee and sandwiches with birdlike, nervous movements while her bent, weary-looking husband hitched the fresh team.

"How's Mr. Tanner?" the old woman asked.

"Fine," Shelter said and the woman smiled. A quick, weary smile.

"He gave us this post when we had nothing, you know." Giles grunted and swallowed his coffee. He had heard this all a hundred times before.

"We had a farm south of Arroyo Grande. The Apaches drove us out, but truthfully, if they hadn't done it the weather would have. To see your corn withered and brown, to watch the soil crack and never, never a drop of rain falling from the hard white skies—well, it became more than a person could bear."

64

Giles grunted a request and she refilled his coffee cup.

"We had a place in Illinois, but Charles wanted to come West. We didn't know. We just didn't know what the conditions were here. We sunk every last cent into that place. Fools that we were," she sighed.

The woman smiled, watching her husband through the open door as he finished hitching the horses to the coach. "Charles likes this. People have told us it's foolish at our age. It's dangerous, they say—that's what Mr. Tanner himself warned us, isn't it, Mel?"

"Yeah," Mel Giles grunted, helping himself to another sandwich.

"But," she said as she smiled weakly at Shelter, "what are we to do? Charles says we can't run all our lives, afraid of shadows. Well, a person can't, do you think?"

"No," Shelter said.

Giles got to his feet, his chair scraping back along the floor. "Let's get going, Morgan."

Shelter rose as well and walked to the stagecoach, the tiny woman waddling behind them, waving and calling up cheerfully, "We'll see you next time. Be careful now."

Giles grimaced and spat. Lifting a hand he snapped the reins and the horses drew them forward, out onto the lonesome desert again, leaving two old, proud people behind.

"Next stop should be Gila Junction," Giles said, "but it got burned out a month ago. Abandoned now. Tanner thinks he'll find some-

65

one to take the station eventually. Small chance, I say. There's only so many goddamned idiots in the world."

The fresh horses wanted to run but Giles held them back. There would be no change of teams at Gila Junction and it was a long way yet to Fort Thomas.

Dawn found them in brush country. Miles of head-high sage and sumac spread out across the convoluted terrain, and to their left the hulking mesa, crowned with gold at the pinnacle, deep in shadow at its base, rose from the land.

"I don't like this stretch," Giles offered. "Too easy for Apaches to hide in this brush. You couldn't see an army until it was too late."

The sun was in Giles's eyes now. Shell kept his hat low, his head turned as he squinted ahead, looking for any shadow, any form that did not seem to belong.

Once, far off, they saw smoke rising into the crystalline skies. Indian smoke. But what it meant, neither knew.

Gila Junction was a collapsed adobe building where blackened timbers jutted up from the rubble. Giles drew into the station warily.

"There's water at least," he explained. He and Shelter stood guard while the horses drank. The scent of ashes was in the air. Two unmarked, fresh graves stood near the pond.

Leaving Gila Junction with the sun directly overhead, they began the last dusty stretch toward Fort Thomas. Giles had loosened up quite a bit. Was it because they were on the last leg, or because the man knew they would not be hit by the Guthries?

Heat waves shimmered across the white sand desert. The land rose and tilted. They had to crest a line of white, sun-blistered hills where nothing at all grew. Giles slowed the horses for the grade.

Shell was looking to the north, peering into the harsh glare as they made a sharp "U" bend in the trail. There was a blur of red and brown, a piercing scream, and the first Apache leaped from the rocks.

Shelter's rifle came up and he fired from the hip. The Apache spun around and fell beneath the coach as Giles laid the whip to the weary horses.

An arrow from somewhere ahead of them whizzed through the air and thudded into the wood of the box between Giles and Shelter.

Shelter crouched down low and Giles followed suit. A flurry of shots sang overhead, one bullet whining off the metal luggage rack, whistling off into the distance.

There were three Apaches across the road and a low line of rocks. Shelter grabbed the shotgun and drew back both hammers. The explosion was deafening.

Shell fired directly over the panicked team's ears and the load of double-aught buckshot ripped the fleeing Apaches to shreds.

One man went down, clawing at his bloody face. A second took off at a run, dragging a leg. The third never moved, he lay crumpled against the earth, his blood staining the white sand.

"Hold on!" Giles yelled. He was going to take the stage over the rock barrier. They might not make it, but he, like Shelter, had visions of being gutted alive and staked out on the desert. Any risk beat being taken by the Indians.

They hit the rocks at full speed and the stage vaulted into the air, tipping crazily, floating through the air for an incredible length of time before it slammed to the earth again, going up on two wheels.

The horses rushed on, lathered, wild-eyed, and the stage swung crazily from side to side. Shelter could do nothing but hang on, and hang on he did as the coach somehow landed upright and jolted on, raising a sea of dust behind them. Fine white powder that rose like smoke against the skies, concealing their pursuit.

But there was pursuit. As the dust slowly filtered earthward Shelter, kneeling on the seat, facing the rear, saw the flashes of color—a red headband, a blue sash, and the driving forms of fresh Indian ponies. A bullet rang out and Shelter, settling down with his Winchester, placed the bead of his sight over the chest of the Apache leader.

The coach hit a bump and he waited. The Apaches drew nearer with each yard they traveled. They screamed, shaking their rifles in anger at the fleeing stage. Shelter waited.

The front sight wavered and he fired, seeing the instant flood of crimson across the bronzed chest of the lead Apache. He fired again, missed, ducked low as an arrow nearly took his hat off, fired again. He watched as a dust-whitened pony crumpled up, throwing its rider, tripping the horses behind.

He fired again, and again, the rifle growing

warm in his hands, and then they were around a bend in the road, among great stacks of gray-white boulders, and the Apaches were gone.

Giles didn't slow the horses until they were salt-flecked and shambling with exhaustion. They had reached the greasewood-studded plain below. Ahead, standing like a dark cube against the pale earth stood Fort Thomas and the surrounding hog town.

The wind was dry and harsh, lifting clouds of sand. The coach lurched along on a twisted undercarriage. Shell sat back, took a deep breath, and grinned at Mel Giles.

"Hell, I don't know what all the fuss is about. This business is a piece of cake." Then he reached out and broke off the protruding arrow, tossed it overboard and leaned back, taking a deep, slow breath.

They rolled into Thomas and Giles steered expertly toward the rented compound where Tanner Line kept a spare coach and three teams. A club-footed hostler came out to meet them.

"Rough one, Mel?"

"Piece of cake," Giles said without a smile. "This here's Morgan, Barney."

"Welcome aboard," Barney said with a nod. He walked around the horses, looking at their lathered flanks with dismay.

"Come on," Mel said. "We'll eat and take care of business."

They ate surprisingly well in the enlisted man's grub hall and then walked across the parade ground where a squad was going through mounted drill.

Shelter followed Mel into the orderly room where a bulldog-faced master sergeant sat lethargically scanning the papers on his desk.

"Captain Lear in?" Giles asked.

The sergeant gave them a slow appraising glance, one of contempt reserved for civilians, and he rose, knocking at the door beside his desk. He leaned his head in and they heard him say, "Those Tanner Line men, sir."

"Send them in."

The sergeant nodded to Giles and Shelter and they walked into the small, hot office. Lear was at the window, watching the drill and the distant desert. He was young for his rank and revealed a limp when he moved to them to shake hands.

"Sit down, gentlemen," Lear offered. He himself perched on the corner of his desk. "I didn't know if I'd be seeing anyone from Tanner again or not."

"It's getting a little thin," Giles admitted.

"So I hear. I was surprised to receive this shipment for you." The captain asked them pointblank, "How long can Tanner hold on?"

"Until they bury the old man, I guess," Giles said.

"Yes." The captain nodded. "That's the only way to defeat Tanner, isn't it?" He told them, "The gold is at the armory. I can give you an escort to Gila Junction, if you like."

"I'd like nothing better," Giles said. "We got hit again, up in the Chalks." He explained about the Apache attack and before he had finished Lear had his first sergeant in the office and a patrol forming.

70

"For all the good it will do. The bastards will be long gone. They're ghosts out there. I've fought Sioux and Arapaho, but I've never seen anything like the Apache. Can't find 'em, can't pin them down and when you do, you only end up sorry."

"Any passengers?" Giles asked as they rose to leave.

The captain gave them a wry smile, "Are you kidding, Mr. Giles?"

"Word gets around, I expect."

"It does."

Shelter followed Giles to the armory and they handed over the captain's authorization to a red-faced corporal. The gold was loaded on the fresh stage by two enlisted men under Giles's watchful eye, and within the hour they were back on the desert with an armed escort of six cavalrymen.

At the Chalks—those white, rocky hills—the escort turned back, leaving them to sit the crest of the hills, a hot wind stirring white dust in the distance and Giles said, "Now the fun begins."

They walked the team forward down the long slope. At the rock barrier Giles let Shelter down to clear the road. The Apache had taken their dead and wounded and vanished into the sands.

There was no indication that there had been a skirmish except for the maroon stains on the rocks.

The sun was in their eyes again as they hit the flats. Giles kept the horses to an evenly paced run. Shelter had drawn up his bandanna to keep the dust from his mouth and nose.

The hours passed slowly, but everything seemed to be going smoothly. Perhaps Tanner was right. The Guthrie gang wouldn't normally suspect another gold shipment this soon. Shelter began to feel ashamed of himself for having suspected Giles of feeding information to the Guthries.

But everything was not all right.

They pulled into Gila Junction Station at sunset. Giles removed his hat, wiped his brow and smiled with relief.

"First leg down."

He clambered down, keeping the reins, and walked the horses toward the pond. Shell followed, stretching his legs. The team was unharnessed and led to water, but already Shelter knew.

Some indefinable sixth sense warned him before his conscious mind reasoned it out. "Hold those horses back, Mel," he said.

"I'll be damned! What the hell's the matter with you?" Giles was having a tough time holding the thirsty horses.

Shelter went to the edge of the pond, dipped a handful of water and tasted it. Rising he told Giles. "It's been poisoned."

"What the hell are you talking about?"

"It's poisoned. Kerosene, I'd say."

Giles knelt down beside the pond and tasted it himself. Acrid, poisonous, oily.

"Ah, bullshit," he said softly. He remained on his knees for a while, and then his head came slowly around. "We got us a problem, Morgan."

"That we do."

It was fifty miles of desert with no water and a weary team, with Apaches on the prowl and a vicious gang of hold-up artists lurking. It was, as Giles said, a problem.

6

They limped on, into the fading sundown. The horses were dragging already and Giles had to slow them to a walk. Shadows crept out of the ravines and flooded the desert. An owl glided past, cutting a brief silhouette against the pale pink and deep purple of the sky.

"They hit us now and we're cooked," Giles said unnecessarily. The thought had been riding with Shelter since Gila Bend.

They were out on the middle of the salt flats, visible for miles, virtually defenseless. They couldn't outrun a healthy horsefly.

"Just keep 'em moving," Shelter said softly.

His mind was turning over another facet of the problem. The pond had been poisoned. All right, why? The answer seemed to be obvious. Someone knew they had gold aboard again.

Shelter glanced at Giles, unable to read his dust-streaked, solemn face. Was it Giles? It seemed it had to be, but there was no way of being sure.

The pale moon rose and sketched crooked shadows before the plodding horses. The desert was still, the night growing frigid. They walked on for hour after hour, nerves raw, expecting the attack at any moment.

"We might make it, by God," Giles said finally. "We just might make it to the next stop."

And it began to seem they might. As the night swept slowly past, the stars wheeling in the skies, the moon growing bright and cold as it reached its zenith.

It was then that Giles drew the coach up sharply, the brake squealing, the horses fighting the bit. Shelter glanced at him angrily.

"What in hell are you doing?"

"Look." Giles's wavering finger pointed skyward and Shell too saw it. A pale line of smoke rose from the dark flats and bled across the face of the moon.

"Get on down there, quick," Shelter said.

"Go to hell!"

"Someone's hit the station!"

"Yeah and what can we do about it?" Giles argued hotly.

"I don't know. Let's see."

"I tell you we can't go down there!"

"We sure as hell can't go back, Giles."

Giles stubbornly refused until Shell came up with the clincher to his argument. The sound of his Colt cocking was loud in the night.

"Get on down."

Giles nodded slowly and he clicked his tongue, walking the stage forward. It took half an hour at that pace and when they got there the ashes were already cold, the defeat complete.

The old man lay near the stable, his head blown away. In the sycamores they found the old woman, that cheerful, forward-looking woman, her throat cut. Giles was sick on the sand.

The horses were gone, the house burned, the coaches overturned and smashed. Shelter crossed to the spring and checked the water, already knowing what he would find. He returned to Giles who was ghastly pale in the moonlight and told him: "The water's poisoned. Kerosene dumped in it."

"Jesus," Giles said softly. He looked up at Shell, eyes bright. "I don't care any more. Beyond a point your pride doesn't matter. When we get to Adobe Falls I'm quitting Tanner."

If, Shell thought, if they got to Adobe Falls.

He was worried now. The Guthries, or whoever was behind this, were not merely trying for the gold, although that would fall into their hands like a ripe plum. They were breaking Tanner.

There was no water at Gila Bend, no station here. The eastern half of the Tanner Line was effectively buried. And there was nothing, nothing whatever Shelter could do about it.

Giles was frozen with indecision and fear. He sat with his head buried in his hands. He was, Shell decided, either a damn fine actor or plenty scared.

"Hitch 'em up, Giles," Shelter said, shaking his shoulder roughly. "Let's go."

"Go," he repeated. "Go where?"

"I don't know, but we can't sit here. Even if the horses drop dead in the traces, we'll be nearer to Adobe Falls."

"It's useless. Let's bury the gold here," he said rising abruptly, excitement on his face. He clutched at Shelter's shirt sleeves.

"No."

"Why not? We can cut us out two horses, maybe make Crater."

"No!" Shelter repeated. "If we do that we'll lose the gold. If we leave it, Tanner's done. If he can't keep his scheduled deliveries up, he's broken and you know it."

"He's done anyway, Morgan! Dammit, can't you see that? We'll never make it."

"We can try." Shell shook free of Giles's grasping hands and slowly backed the weary team up to the coach, hitching them as Giles sat on the ground, peering through his fingers at Shelter Morgan.

Shell returned to the man and, crouching, asked, "Isn't there water somewhere nearer than Adobe Falls? Anywhere?"

"No. There's nothing."

"Think, goddammit!"

He shook Giles and Giles, amazingly, answered instantly: "Wild Horse Spring."

"How far is it?"

"Too far. Twenty miles."

"We can't make it without water to Adobe Falls."

"I know," Giles said miserably.

"Then let's try for Wild Horse Spring."

"You don't understand—there's not always water there. And . . . the Apaches use it."

"They'll have to share with us then," Morgan

76

said with steely determination. "Come on, Giles. You've got one more night's guts in you."

"Yeah." He shook his head as if it weighed a ton and came wearily to his feet. "I'll try it. Once more. But this is it. I'm telling Tanner tonight."

"Sure. You do that."

"See if I don't," Giles grumbled. He walked to the coach, clambered up, and with a slow, painful shake of his head he coaxed the exhausted team into motion.

They glided across the salt flats, glimmering silver in the fading moonlight. They passed the black, weird forms of ocotillo and giant saguaro. Giles veered off the road, his face stony as he drove. They were three miles from the road when it happened.

Giles yanked on the reins, drew his six-gun and emptied it in the direction of a cactus. Shelter lunged at him, slamming his fist into Giles's face. He tore the revolver from the driver's hand and flung it out onto the desert. The echoes of the shots still rolled across the flats.

"Why'd you hit me?" Giles whimpered. He had his face turned away, a shoulder lifted protectively. "Why'd you hit me?"

"Are you crazy!" Shelter growled. "Plain crazy, Giles?"

"I thought I saw an Indian."

"You thought . . . damn you, you fool! You didn't see anything, but by God you've told everyone on this desert exactly where we are, haven't you?"

They rode on glumly, the moon sinking below

the mountain range, darkness swallowing up the desert. Shelter was more than a little worried now, more than a little suspicious.

That exhibition of Giles's was something other than panic. Or so it seemed to Morgan. A prearranged signal? And to whom? He didn't trust Giles, never had. Now he didn't take his eyes off the sullen stage driver.

The coach moved at a walk, the springs creaking, the harnesses popping occasionally as a horse stumbled. "How far?" Shelter asked finally.

"A mile," Giles answered, his voice a hoarse crack. Maybe, Shell thought looking at the man, maybe I was too hasty. The man genuinely appeared petrified with fear, his nerve broken. Shelter had seen a few, during the war, and damn him if Giles's fear didn't seem real now.

They found it, and miraculously there was water there. Sweet, cool water and the horses were led to it, taken away before they drank too much, and led back again. Shelter filled his canteen by starlight and watched Giles immerse himself in the water.

He rose shakily, trying for a grin which would not come.

"I'm sorry, Morgan. I guess I've just had enough of this. I'm coming apart all at once."

Shelter only nodded. "Let's hitch 'em up," he said and Giles agreed quickly.

They returned to the road by a different course, riding at an even pace beneath a cool, starlit sky, the breeze fresh against their bodies.

Giles swung westward once again and Shell

began to relax a little. Ten miles to Adobe Falls, no more. Then Tanner could decide what he wanted to do—push on to Tucson or not. With a fresh driver, Reyes perhaps, they could still make the schedule.

He was thinking that way when he saw the orange haze against the dark horizon and realized that there was a fire and that the fire could only be in one place.

"Whip those sons of bitches!" Shelter said. "They're burning Adobe Falls."

Giles froze, hypnotized by the flames, by fear. Then Shelter yelled again and he did whip them, coming to his feet.

"Hee-yaw!" Giles hollered and the horses lay back their ears and gave it all they had.

They jolted down into the wash and up through the sycamores. Shelter's eyes searched the bluffs, the buildings, the low brush.

The drivers' bunkhouse was ablaze, flames lighting the entire yard brightly. By that light Shell saw a running dark figure, and he lifted his Winchester.

He fired, missed, muttered a curse, and fired again. The man went down. Shelter's shots drew an answering hail of bullets from the sycamores where the outlaws were positioned.

A rifle from the bluffs, Tanner's sentry, fired into the yard, and from the house stabbing muzzle flames showed intermittently.

A gun barked close by and Giles tilted crazily to the side. Shell clutched at him, missed and saw the driver topple from the box.

79

The coach jolted over his body and Shelter dove for the reins. It was hopeless. There was no way to drive and fight back the vicious attack simultaneously. One of the ribbons had dropped free and the team trampled on it, yanking the wheel horse's head violently to one side.

The coach threatened to roll as the panicked horse wheeled abruptly. But it righted itself and rushed on, unattended through the yard.

A figure loomed out of the darkness, backlighted by the sheet of orange flames, and grabbed for the harness. Shelter shot him in the chest and he was trampled into the earth.

The house, its face peppered with bullet holes, stood only yards from where Shelter now rode the racing team. He saw covering fire laid down from the two front windows and he made his move.

Reaching down he grasped the strongbox and dropped it over the side, dropping free himself at the same time. He hit the earth rolling, bullets whizzing around him, and got to his feet in time to see the stagecoach roll, the tongue break free, the team go galloping off into the fire-bright night.

Shelter rushed for the porch of the house, hitting the planks at a dead run. Bullets tore up splinters at his heels but the door was opened as he reached it, and he dove through, the door slamming behind him as the insane roar of the rifles outside continued.

It might have been Shiloh. The smoke rolled across the yard, obscuring and then revealing the bodies which lay there. The guns racketed from the sycamore trees and the bullets whined off the house. The sky blazed fiercely as if the night itself had caught fire.

"Thank God," Ellie Tanner said and she threw her arms around Shell, clinging to him as the bullets found a pane of glass and sent jagged slivers flying across the room. "Thank God."

Tanner himself sat propped in a wooden chair at the window. His shirt was ripped open, his left arm hanging uselessly at his side. There was blood on his cheek and powder had smoked his face black.

He grinned painfully. "Cut the lolly-gaggin', Morgan. Get to shootin'."

He himself fired with his one good arm, awkwardly levered a fresh cartridge into the chamber, and fired again as a bullet from outside splintered the windowsill.

Moving in a crouch Shell got to the southernmost window. He saw a darting figure, torch in hand, crossing the yard, and he fired, dropping the outlaw in his tracks.

"Atta boy!" Tanner shouted. Then his cry of glee broke off into a blood-strangled cough.

"They're trying the back!" Ellie called from the kitchen. Shelter ran that way to find Ellie firing through a window, trying to check an assault on the back of the house.

He heard the sudden rush of feet on the back porch and they hit the door. They slammed something hard against it and the door shuddered on its hinges. They hit it again, trying to batter it down, to get inside, to kill.

Morgan stood ten feet from the door and with

wild ferocity he held his Winchester waist high and emptied it into the door. His slugs tore splinters from the wood, producing a scream of pain and clouding the room with black smoke.

Ellie was firing from the window, picking off those who lagged making their retreat, and then suddenly it was silent—unbelievably so.

They could hear the crackling of flames as the bunkhouse continued to burn. Also, they heard the low moaning of a man on the back porch as he slowly died. Shell felt no sorrow for the man—he had chosen the wrong game. If they had burst through that door it would have been Ellie who suffered.

"What's happened, where are they?" Ellie asked.

"They didn't like the taste of it," Shelter said, peering through the window. "They'll be trying to figure out a cheap way to get us out of here."

She nodded, biting at her lower lip. A strand of dark hair was draped across her serious face. The girl had guts, he had to give her that.

Impulsively he leaned forward and kissed her neck through the screen of hair and she made a pleased sound, turning her dark, bright eyes to him.

"The strongbox is in the yard," Shell told her, his hand resting on Ellie's shoulder. "It's in plain sight, but that's no advantage to them. We can see anyone crossing the yard. Where's Reyes?" he asked suddenly.

"He's in the blacksmith's shed."

Is, or *was?* Shelter hadn't seen any rifle fire

coming from that shed at all.

"Do you think he's all right?" Ellie asked anxiously.

"Sure. Sure he is," Shell said.

She turned to him, suddenly seeming small and weak. She hugged him tightly, her rifle dangling from one hand, and he felt her sigh deeply.

"This is . . . just a little too much," she said.

"You can handle it," he said with a smile. He stroked her dark hair and she nodded.

"I thought I saw Mel with you."

"You did. They got him."

"He wasn't so bad," she said quietly, turning to look out the window again. "His nerve just went. Suddenly it just went."

"Yours won't."

"No."

"Check on your uncle," Shell said. "I'll watch here."

"He's hurt bad," she replied.

"Sometimes it looks a lot worse than it is," Shelter said.

"Sure." She tried for a smile and lifted herself to tiptoes and kissed him. Then she was gone, a small, quite courageous woman with a big Winchester repeater in her hand.

Shelter turned his attention to the yard. By the still-burning fire he could see the abandoned strongbox, a dull green cube against the red earth. He could also see anybody attempting to reach it, and they knew it.

Yet if they were going to try it, they would have to do it soon. The sun would be slipping above the horizon in a little over an hour. While the fire held they could not attempt it, however.

It must have been frustrating for them to sit and watch, knowing that to move was to die. And then someone did move. A crouched, dark figure slipping through the trees. Shelter fired and the figure disappeared.

There was no answering shot and no more movement. Looking eastward now Shell saw the gray of false dawn, and a little later the soft fading of night, the first golden shaft of sunrise.

Something stirred again in the sycamores. A horse nickered and then Shelter saw them filtering through the trees, riding out onto the desert, a long line of dark men on dark horses. They had given it up for now.

They had given it up, but they had left a man dead, a coach wrecked, a building burned, an old man injured. They had crippled the Tanner Line still more. And they would be back.

Shelter knew it. They would be back; they would not quit until Tanner was smashed. The gold seemed almost secondary and that caused him to wonder. There was something else which caused him to wonder—he saw Fernando Reyes, hat tilted back on his head, striding toward the house, a grin of relief on his face.

Shell walked into the front room where Ellie was working on her uncle's arm, bandaging it. Willie's face was knotted with pain. His wounds were bad, very bad.

Fernando Reyes stepped into the room, grinning.

"Beat them back, by God! Chased them right out of here."

"All but one," Shelter said softly.

Ellie's head came up. Her lips were pursed quizzically. "What do you mean, Shell?"

"Ask Fernando what I mean."

"I don't get you, Morgan," Reyes said, shrugging.

"I think you do. You're one of 'em, Reyes."

7

No one moved for a long moment. Willie Tanner's glazed eyes lifted to Shelter, and Ellie's lips compressed harshly. Her hand froze in midair as she wrapped a clean bandage around her uncle's arm.

"What's the matter, Shelter Morgan?" Fernando Reyes asked. "What made you crazy? Everybody knows Fernando. Me, I'm a Tanner man."

"No." Shell shook his head. "There had to be a man inside for the Guthries to know when the gold was being shipped. Mel Giles had been here for years, but the trouble only started recently. How long have you been here, Fernando?" There was no answer. Shell went on.

"Anyway, Mel is dead, that kind of lets him out."

"I have to die to prove I'm innocent!" Fernando said, spreading his hands. He grinned ironically at Ellie.

"Shell," the girl said, "you must be wrong."

"Am I? Think about this—I was out there during the battle. Fernando was in the blacksmith's shed? There were no shots fired from that shed. He wasn't fighting them off. He was lying back having a cigarette, counting up the money he was making while you were getting shot to pieces."

"Incredible!" Reyes said, waving a hand. He shook his head and turned away. Shelter began to think maybe he was wrong. He thought that until Reyes spun, his hand dropping toward his Colt. Reyes was quick. He turned, his face twisted into contemptuous triumph.

Reyes got his shot off first, but Shelter had drawn, and as Reyes's gun exploded in the close confines of the room, spewing fire and death, his burnt gunpowder rolling in a cloud across the room, Shelter drew and his Colt bucked three times in his hand.

The first bullet tagged Reyes high on the shoulder, spinning him around. The second tore the guts out of the man and he screamed, slumping to the floor, his Colt dangling from his fingers. Shelter shot again, fully conscious of what he was doing, anger flaring up hotly in him.

Reyes was hammered to the floor and he lay there, blood leaking from him, staining the floorboards crimson.

Shell hovered over him, gun still in his fist, and then he turned back to face an astonished Ellie. Willie Tanner was sagged in his chair, his face waxen, his eyes empty.

"I'm glad—I'm glad you—"

And then he said no more. He went soft, his head lolling to one side, his last breath gasping from his lungs.

"Uncle Willie! Uncle Willie!" Ellie slapped his hand and took his face between her palms, shaking it from side to side, her shrieks rising in intensity until she realized beyond doubt that he was dead. Only then did she let her hands slowly slip away.

"He's gone," she said quietly. She shrugged, touched her hair and staggered toward Shelter. "He's really gone. I didn't think they could do it. I didn't think . . ."

And Shelter had to hold her, to let her cling to him while the tears flowed and the sobbing rose and finally ebbed, leaving her shrunken, exhausted. Ellie sagged into a chair, staring at the floor.

"They tried to scare him and when he wouldn't scare they tried to burn us out, to destroy Tanner. And when that wasn't enough . . ."

He thought she was going to cry again, but she seemed to take on resolution. She shook her hair, took a slow breath and, looking steadily at Morgan, said, "Well, they haven't won yet. Damn them! They haven't beaten us yet."

She turned then and walked into the kitchen, and after a minute he heard her banging pots and pans around. And a long while after, he heard the sound of her sobbing.

Shelter worked in the soft sand beneath the sycamores, his shirt hanging on a tree branch. The shovel *shooshed* into the sand as he silently, methodically dug the graves. The sun was hot on his back and the gnats plagued his ears, eyes, and nostrils.

Finally he was through. Nothing remained of these men's lives but sad humps of damp sand. He straightened up and drew on his shirt.

Shelter took a ride northward, searching for and finding the dead sentry. He had fallen fifty feet from the top of the bluff and there was nothing human remaining about the twisted, broken body. He caved the bluff in over the man and returned to the house.

He smelled coffee as he entered, barring the door behind him. The strongbox rested in the middle of the floor which had been scrubbed again. There was no blood, no sign of death.

Shelter went into the kitchen, but Ellie was not there. He poured himself a cup of black, steaming coffee and sipped at it, watching morning come to the desert through the shattered window.

"Shell?"

He turned his head and there stood Ellie.

Her hair was down around her shoulders and she was completely naked. Her ripe breasts bobbed as she walked toward him. Her eyes seemed glazed. Her full hips were fluid. His eyes swept over her, pausing at the dark triangle between her sturdy thighs.

"I want you to make love to me," she said. She stood inches from him, her breasts at the level of his lips.

Shell shook his head. "You're distraught."

"Yes!" her voice rose shrilly. *"Distraught!"* She ran her fingers through her hair and closed her eyes, arching her back so that her breasts were thrust out even more prominently.

She quieted herself. "You're a good man, Shell. I know you are. You don't want to take advantage of me, to use me. But you won't be, you see. I want to use you! I want you to love me, to drive away all of this . . . all of these memories. Let's be alive, Shell! The others—they have died."

And slowly she slipped onto his lap, drawing his head to her breasts. He took her taut, pink nipple into his mouth and felt the electric tingling of her body.

She clung to him, and her fingers slowly unbuttoned his shirt as her breasts rose and fell with almost hysterical excitement.

She kissed his neck, tugged his shirt from his waistband, and let her hands roam the expanse of his chest, her leg quivering as Shell's hand slipped onto her thigh and slowly stroked her.

Their mouths met, hers eager, warm, moist. And Shell stood, holding the kiss as he did so. Ellie yanked his shirt down his arms, her breath rapid, her eyes bright. Then she worked on his belt buckle, growing angry when she had difficulty with it.

Finally it was undone, and as Shelter kissed her smooth shoulder, she unbuttoned his fly, her hands dipping inside as his trousers fell to the floor.

"Oh, my," she sighed, and she was content to stand there for a moment, feeling the pulsing warmth of his erection against her palms, stroking the length of him, her own legs quivering with emotion as Shelter's hands gently, slowly spread her, finding the rigid tab of soft flesh between her legs.

"God," she sighed and sagged against him, spreading her legs as she clung to his cock. Her mouth opened with slack-jawed amazement, and her eyes were half-closed; she became lost in some netherland of sensation as his strong hands touched her, as his mouth roamed her breasts, dropped to her abdomen, as she clung to him, wanting to straddle him, to ride him to forgetfulness.

"The bedroom," she said, and her voice was a panting, urgent plea.

She turned, taking Shell's hand and he smiled. "Just a minute."

He sat and kicked off his boots, pulling his trousers off as Ellie stood, eyes fixed on his erection, all the savage maleness of Shelter Morgan. She fidgeted as if she could not stand still another minute and when he rose she again clung to him, her hands kneading his hard buttocks, her mouth smeared against his.

They walked quickly through the front room and into her tiny, windowless bedroom where Ellie closed and barred the door and lay back on the brass bed. She had folded back the quilt and Shelter could see her dresses, her petticoats, her jeans thrown around the room.

Now he concentrated on Ellie, however. She had her head on the pillow, her legs drawn up, knees spread—and her fingers toyed with her crotch, opening herself to his view. Her smile was erotic, childish, and pleading all at once as she tucked an exploring finger between her thighs, her other hand stretching out, grasping for Shelter Morgan who moved to the side of the bed, offering her his erection which she encircled with her small, warm hand. She continued to stroke herself, her knees spread wide, her mouth open in sensual slackness.

"Now," she panted, and her thighs quivered, her eyes dilated, her tongue touched her lips. "Now, now, now." And she drew him to her, her hands closing around his erection, slipping between his thighs to cup and heft the heavy sack there.

Her hips began to lift and sway as if she had no control over them and she drew Shelter down, touching the sensitive head of his cock to her flame-red, quivering clitoris. She ran the tip of his erection up and over it, her throat forming tiny, grunting sounds of deep, draining pleasure, and then suddenly she thrust the head of his cock inside of her, and she was grabbing at him, tugging at his scrotum, clawing at his buttocks as she grappled with him, swallowing him up with her warm, fluid inner flesh which craved him, clenched at him.

Then Shelter began to move against her and he thrust it home, filling her until her mouth opened in soundless pain, soundless pleasure, until she felt him scraping her spine, felt him swelling inside of her, driving all of the evil away, all of the terrible memories.

Shell got to his knees, his hands slipping beneath her smooth white buttocks, and he lifted her against him as he rocked back, swaying against her. He saw himself entering the pink, glistening smoothness of her, saw the trembling muscles of her thighs, the hollows where her legs met her crotch, the sweep of her softly rounded abdomen, quivering with sensation, the mounds of her abundant breasts crowned with taut nipples.

Her mouth was partly open, her head rolling from side to side, her eyes squinting as if in deepest concentration.

And constantly there was the thrust of her hips, the rise and fall, the sway, the pitch of her pelvis against him as her body offered itself upon an altar of need, offered itself to be split, cloven, tilted, and penetrated, used as a refuge, opened wide, ground to nerveless, grateful flesh.

Shelter worked against her, lifting her buttocks, driving into her, feeling the contours, the ridges and protuberances of her inner sheath which accommodated him so eagerly, so demandingly.

Her hands dropped between her legs, crept through the soft, dark bush which flourished there and found his cock driving into her. She fastened her fingers around it, her breath coming in tiny, amazed gasps.

Shelter felt the rush of fluid within her, and he felt the tightening of her fingers, the probing, groping fingers with which she touched herself, touched Shelter, trying to make them one, stroking his man-flesh and her own bursting womanhood as he swayed against her.

His hands gripped the soft half globes of her buttocks with tenacious strength. He drove his pelvis against hers, heard the soft laugh, the small cries exiting her throat as tears flooded her cheeks, as her hips drummed against the bed. She tore at him, reaching an incredible, dewy climax moments before Shelter threw himself forward, pressing his chest against her breasts, molding his mouth to hers, feeling her tongue dart between his lips. As he quickened his cadence, he felt her legs lift, her heels rest on his ass as he filled her with a sudden wild climax. Then the wild rhythm fell away to a soft, anticlimactic pulsing of two bodies working against each other, seeking the last gentle drop of pleasure.

It seemed a very long time that they lay there, Ellie's fingertips running up and down Shelter's spine, tracing the cleft of his buttocks, her lips touching his shoulders, throat, mouth, and cheeks, but it couldn't have been more than a few minutes.

"We have to go," she said. Her voice was calmer now, filled with resolve.

Shelter rolled to one side, his eyes fixed on hers, his finger sketching patterns around her nipple.

"Where? Crater?"

"What for? she said. "That's no good." She nipped his shoulder playfully and she tightened her thighs, gripping his still-erect shaft.

"The law's there."

"Snowden!" She made a disparaging noise. Shell nipped at her breast and she was silent a moment, her hand in his dark hair.

"Don't you like him? Or don't you think he's honest?" Shelter asked.

"No."

He grinned. "Where then? What is it you want to do, little one?"

94

"Keep Tanner on schedule," she said.

Shelter paused. His hand cupped her breast, his lips which had been kissing her soft throat formed into a quizzical line.

"You're not joking?"

"Of course not. What is all of this worth if Tanner is broken? I want to take that gold through to Tucson, Shelter Morgan."

"You know they're out there—the Guthries. You know we haven't got a dog's chance of getting through."

"Yes. But at least we'll go out happy," she said, placing the back of her hand against his cheek. "You've seen to that."

"I'm not quite ready to go out yet, myself," Shell answered. She pushed away from him with both hands.

"You mean you won't help me?"

"No, I don't mean that. Of course I'll help you. Ellie?" he asked, "that isn't why—?"

"No." She smiled. "The reason is I needed you, and you're a great stud animal, Shelter Morgan. You're a little rough, you know." She kissed the tip of his nose. "But gentle too. I think you're a hell of a man," she said, and Shelter sighed with relief. He didn't want her saying what she had in her mind.

He was silent, pondering the problem. To get through to Tucson with that gold, you'd need an army. Assuming he did get through, what good would it do? The next trip would be just as hard, and the next.

A conviction began to solidify in his mind.

There was only one way to save the Tanner Line and that was to go after them. To become the aggressor, to wipe out the Guthries before they could destroy what was left of the business. He knew that it was his job to do. They had killed an old man, and now they would destroy this woman's means of livelihood, or worse. . . .

"I'll try it after dark," Shelter said.

"You! *We*, Mr. Morgan. We'll try it." Ellie Tanner protested.

"You can't go out there. You know what they'll try. It's no secret that we've got the gold, no secret that you control the lines now."

"That's right. I am the Tanner Lines." She sat up. "How can I run from my responsibility? I can handle a team, Mr. Morgan—handle a team in a way you can't imagine."

"Too damned hazardous," Shell objected.

"No it's not. It's hazardous for you to try to drive and fight at once. With me driving and you riding shotgun we've got our best chance."

"Ellie," he asked, "do you really want to do this? Is it some wild idea of loyalty to your uncle? If they catch us out there they'll cut our throats, and you know it. Think about it."

"I have," she said pertly. She tilted her head to one side. "Are you working for me still or not?"

He grinned, drew her down to him and whispered, "Still working for you, Miss Tanner. What's my first assignment?" His hand rested on her hip and now began to crawl up her thigh.

"Later for that, hombre," she laughed. "And I do mean later." Her seriousness returned. "We have to try it, Shell. No. I don't mean that. We have to *make* it. Trying isn't good enough."

"All right. Listen, if there's an alternate route, let's take that, even if it's the long way around. They'll no doubt have someone watching us from the moment we leave, but maybe if we take off under cover of darkness we can confuse them. We'll leave early, before the moon rises."

"An hour after dark."

"Fine. Where's the nearest station?" he asked.

"Dog Creek—but there's no one there."

That was where Ellie's parents had been killed, he recalled.

"And after that?"

"Troubadour. That's a hundred miles off. Jack Upton was holding it down up until last week. Maybe he's still there."

"All right, we'll plan on Troubadour. The problem is anyone who wants to hit the coach knows the route, knows where the horses have to be changed. I propose we try it a little differently. Set up a new route in effect."

"But without fresh horses and water!"

"We'll save the horses. Water we can carry. There are no passengers so we can stand the extra weight. You've got a water barrel, don't you? Yes, I saw one in the blacksmith's shed out back of the house. We'll lash them inside the coach and fill them. That should see us through to Troubadour, don't you think?"

"There's no way through!" Ellie put a nervous hand to her forehead. "When we laid out the route, Uncle Willie used the only pass through the mountains."

"There has to be another way," Shelter urged.

"Not suitable for a stagecoach."

"Think!"

"There's only Carson Pass and the road there's nothing but a game path. I suppose if a person was desperate enough . . ."

"We are, Ellie. If we don't cross the Guthries up, we've bought our own death."

"Well, it could be taken. But my God, Shelter, it's an Apache stronghold up there!" She sagged back against the bed and he took her hand.

"Maybe they're not there now. You know the Apaches—they never stay in one place."

"I don't know. I'm just not sure. Maybe it can't be done, Shell, maybe it's all a crazy dream."

"It can be done, Ellie," he told her sincerely. "There's damn little that can't be done if a man gets down to it. We'll give it our best, girl, and if it doesn't work out—well, they won't be able to say we didn't try."

"Sure!" she brightened. "You can do it. You can make it work, Shelter. You'll get me through."

"Of course," he answered, patting her shoulder. Morgan can get you through. Morgan can make a bull fly. "Get dressed," he said, managing a smile. "And let's have at it."

8

Dusk was slow in settling. The sun seemed to linger in the sky tauntingly. There was nothing left to do. The coach with the fresh team stood behind the house, the strongbox strapped into the boot. Two fifty-gallon water barrels rested in the passenger compartment, fastened in place with old harness straps nailed to the floor and walls of the coach.

Now there was nothing to do. Nothing but watch the slowly settling purple dusk flood the desert. The flight of a low-winging dove cut brief, hectic silhouettes against the sky. Ellie was at his elbow, her hands encased in driving gloves. She wore a curled black hat and a six-gun. She was trying to look brave and not making a good show of it. Shelter hugged her tightly and she smiled.

They stood there until full dark, Shelter's eyes scouring the darkness. The Guthries would be there, somewhere. They had too much invested in this robbery attempt to quit now.

When he could no longer see Ellie's face beside his, Shelter whispered, "Let's have at it. It's as dark as it's going to get."

The stars were bright in a blue-black sky. The rising bluffs stood black and mute. The trees shifted in the breeze. Ellie climbed into the driver's seat, Shelter beside her.

"This is the worse part," Shelter said and she nodded.

"Here goes." She snapped the reins and the team moved out at a dead slow walk, crossing the empty yard of the Adobe Falls station. Ellie stayed low as Shelter had advised her, but she was ready to whip that team into a run if need be.

They made it to the sycamores where Shelter half-expected to be hit, and then out onto the open desert. Shell released the breath he had been holding.

"Take the regular road," he said and she nodded. Ellie was rigid with apprehension, and she had every right to be.

The desert was silent, the saw-toothed mountains standing against the cold night sky as they had for eons. The trace chains had been padded with torn rags, and there was only the creak of harness leather, the soft plodding of the horses' hooves.

The coach dipped into the dry bed of Finger Creek and was temporarily lost in the thicket of willow brush. It was here that Ellie had suggested they leave the main road. Now, with a glance at Shelter, she turned the team southward.

It was completely dark, only starlight glinting on the shifting willows. Any observer would have a tough time seeing that the coach had turned off the main road.

Two miles downstream Ellie brought the team up onto the flats. Shell shifted in the seat, peering out at the blank face of the limitless desert, seeing no one. "Hold up a minute," Shell said and Ellie did so.

He sat there in the silence, listening, hearing nothing at all in the night. "All right, let's go," Shell told her.

For the moment there seemed nothing to fear. He glanced toward the mountains, wondering what was in store for them up there—a broken trail, prowling Apaches—and he wondered again what he was doing involved in this. There was an answer, of course, it was the only decent thing a man could do.

He had not really spoken much with Ellie before now. While things were quiet he took the opportunity to ask about Du Rose.

"No," she shook her head, "there's no one like that living around here . . . wait a minute." She turned toward him, starlight in her eyes. "I did see someone. I couldn't be sure it was the same man, of course. But a man who looked like that stopped at Adobe Falls once."

"What did he want?"

"He wanted to talk to Fernando," she remembered. Shell heard a sharp intake of breath. "Who is he? What would he want?"

"He's a criminal, Ellie. As to what he wanted, I couldn't say." A thought came to him. "Have you actually seen old Jeremiah Guthrie? Do you know what he looks like?"

"Oh, yes." She shuddered. "A huge, bald, cranky old man. Nearly toothless. This Du Rose of yours, he's not Jeremiah Guthrie, if that's what you were thinking."

"It was. Most of these men have changed their names."

"But you always find them anyway."

"Some. I've had some luck." The stage hit a chuckhole and Shell bounced into the air a few inches.

"Is that what you do—hunt down people? What are you, a law officer?"

"That's what I do," he said grimly. "No, I'm not an officer of the law. I went to the law with this and they said there was nothing they could do. I was the only witness, you see, and it was my word against theirs. Assuming the government wanted to try tracking down these people all over the West, and they didn't, not on my say-so.

"I respect the law, Ellie. I respect it when it works, when it does what it's supposed to do. The idea of having law is to protect the innocent, but when it starts protecting the guilty—well, maybe what I'm doing isn't legal, but it's right."

"Do you . . . kill them?" she asked, her throat constricted.

"When they force it. But to answer what you really want to know, I haven't set myself up as an executioner, no. Most of these men have been engaged in criminal activities. It seems once you start down that trail it's hard to get off it. I'm proud to say I've seen some of them locked up. Some of them have tried to kill me. That was their choice."

She didn't have to ask what had happened to them. Shelter was here and they, presumably, were not. They rode silently after that, with Shelter turning various possibilities around in his head. There was something to all of this business beyond simple robbery and he was beginning to have an inkling as to what it was. A couple of small points that had bothered Morgan began to make more sense.

"There it is," Ellie said, and Shelter's head lifted.

The rising moon illuminated a rough trail winding into the bleak, jagged mountains. He whistled softly. "That's rough, isn't it?"

"Want to turn back?" Ellie asked with a smile.

"To where?" Shelter asked. They'd be lucky if Adobe Falls was standing now. "This was your bright idea anyway," he reminded her.

"*That* wasn't." She sighed, lifting her chin toward the rocky broken trail which led into the jagged hills.

"We can do it," Shelter said with a smile. The comment was more a gesture of comfort than a statement of fact. Ellie knew that and she canted her head toward him, kissing his neck, and snapped the reins, once again moving the team forward.

The canyon was a dark yawning chasm, the moonlit trail a silver thread along the sheer denuded bluffs. The coach moved like a wooden insect beneath the sky above. Shelter sat in the box, every sense intent on the night. Guthrie could not be here, could not expect this move; but the Apache could be anywhere, and their survival depended on expecting anything.

Ellie had said these mountains were an Apache stronghold, but Shelter was banking on them not rising up from their beds in the middle of the night to attack a passing stagecoach.

The trail itself was their chief adversary. As it wound higher, the trail narrowed. Twice Shell had to clamber down to clear rockslides, wasting precious time. The drop to their right was a good thousand feet already and they rode half the time with the off-side wheels threatening to drop over the rim.

The moon rode higher, coasting through the star-bright skies. They had reached a sort of plateau where grass grew and a few wind-flagged cedars stood silhouetted against the sky. It was there, while the horses rested and were given water from the barrels, that Shelter heard the chilling sound of an owl.

"Only an owl," Ellie said, seeing Shell tense, watching his eyes search the darkness. But she too knew that it was not a feathered owl; they had been spotted.

"Maybe," she commented in a low voice as if speaking to comfort herself, "it's Indians, but that doesn't mean they'll bother to wake the camp and attack us. After all—what have we got?"

"You're right," Shell agreed. What did they have? Nothing but four good horses, guns, fifty thousand in gold, and a white woman.

The rest was cut short and they walked the team

forward across the dark, empty plateau. Another mile into the hills and they would begin the downward stretch. Once onto the desert they planned to cut northward toward Troubadour, where, with any luck at all Jack Upton was still holding down the Tanner Line station.

The moon had begun to sink behind the ragged hills, and Shelter could feel his nerves jumping. He had met people in the East who still believed an Indian wouldn't attack after dark. He had buried a few greenhorns who had felt that way.

The truth was that an Apache, like any other plundering tribesman, would take any risk if the reward was rich enough. Shell figured what they were carrying was just about enough.

They topped a narrow saddle and began the slow downward slope. The brake squealed too loudly in the night. Shell glanced over and saw the determination on Ellie's face and he had to smile. That was a woman, all five feet of her. Someone like Phoebe Strawn would never understand Ellie. Phoebe would have crumpled up, folded like a wet dishrag by now.

They rounded a sharp "U" in the trail. Now the cliffs rose up two hundred feet or more above them, and the drop to the rocky canyon floor below was three times that.

Shell heard the trickle of sand, turned sharply to his right in time to see the first cream-colored boulder teeter on the rim above and come roaring down the canyon, driving hundreds of smaller rocks before it.

"Ellie! Back 'em up!" he shouted, but she

paused for a minute too long, wanting to know why when there was no time to explain why, no time for anything but instant reaction. She was no soldier, but only a weary, frightened girl and she hesitated. The hesitation cost them.

The gigantic boulder bounced high into the air and Ellie saw it from the corner of her eye. "My God!" she muttered, but still she was frozen. Shell yanked back hard on the reins himself.

"Whoa! Whoa!" he shouted. "Back 'em now, Ellie, dammit, back 'em!"

Ellie spoke to the horses. The still-shuddering weight of the stagecoach was pressing against the team, and although they were well-trained, they couldn't believe, apparently, that the driver actually wanted them to back up a grade.

Ellie fought the reins and the horses balked. Finally the lead horse responded, but it was already too late. The boulder bounced again, and as Shell watched, it slowly turned over in the air and crashed into the horses, sweeping them over the ledge as they whinnied in fear, as the mass of earth and stone rumbled down the gorge.

"Jump, Ellie!" Shelter shouted, but she sat frozen, her eyes wide as two Kansas moons. The earth and rock swept the team away as the stage inexorably followed, tilting up on the left front wheel before slowly rolling into space.

Shelter leaped toward the trail, a head-sized rock hammering his thigh as he fell. The dust billowed skyward and the rocks continued to fall in a mad jumble.

He buried his head beneath his arms as

hundreds of small stones pounded against his back and legs, as tons of earth slid off the bluff, burying him. The coach tilted and rolled off into space, the panicked cries of the horses echoing up the long canyon.

Shelter tried to lift his head and was hammered back. A rock rang off his skull and the night became brighter, the stars going from pale blue to brilliant red before he felt the nausea begin. Then the night went as dark as a coal mine at midnight.

Hours later—or was it only minutes—Morgan felt sharp, distant pain shaking him and demanding his return to consciousness. He started to roll over and found it was impossible. Tons of earth and rock pressed down on him like a black hand.

His skull pounded with a sudden surge of pulse. Trapped! Pinned down, doomed to suffocate.

He forced himself to grow cold, to appraise things logically, to fight down the rising apprehension. Where was Ellie? He hadn't seen her since the coach went over. Dead, alive, in the hands of the Apaches?

"Take it easy, Morgan. One step at a time," he told himself. "Anything broken?"

He couldn't be sure. His right leg was shot through with pain. Both legs were immobilized by stone and earth. He could move his right hand, but his left was twisted back and pinned solidly.

Dust filled his nostrils, ears, and eyes, but there was some sort of air pocket around his head, obviously, or he would have been suffocated by now.

"First things first, my man," he muttered.

The first thing was to free both arms. His right he could wriggle, although its movement was restricted, and with that hand he began digging out.

He found that by twisting his arm and drawing it toward him he could slowly clear it. But how much stone was above him, waiting to cave in? There was no answer. His world was dark, tight, and stifling. One thing mattered—to get the right arm free.

Slowly he did so, dragging rocks into the area next to his head where the air pocket was. Then when his arm was free he cautiously removed the rocks again, returning them to where the arm had been pinned.

"Now," he panted. The air was already rancid, and Shelter's rapid breathing did little to satisfy his burning lungs. Sweat poured from his face, stinging his eyes. "Now to roll . . ." but there was no way to roll. His right hand scrabbled toward his left side, a crablike, useless thing.

"Slowly, boy, slowly," he muttered. His right hand carefully, methodically cleared a head-sized stone and then several smaller ones around his left shoulder. The effort of this contortion flooded his body with pain. His lungs gasped for oxygen which was not there.

His right hand, trickling blood now, cleared the left down to the elbow before life surged back into that arm, the circulation rushing back in waves studded with pins and needles. But both arms were free, no matter that there was no freedom of movement.

"Up and out," he encouraged himself. Up and out—but was it even possible? For all he knew half the mountain was on top of him. There was no other choice but to lie there and die, however, and so he tried it.

He shifted slightly and felt with raw fingers the stones before him. Finding one key rock he tugged, holding his breath, knowing that that move might be the one to bring tons of crushing stone down upon him.

The rock moved, followed by a trickle of earth. And then—by God!—cool, fresh air.

That air, night air moist with dew and ripe with the scent of sage and greasewood, flooded the small hollow where Shelter lay and he let his head fall forward, breathing in deeply, soaking his body with precious oxygen.

"Don't get excited now, son," Shelter reminded himself. He was only under two or three feet of rubble, but his legs were still pinned, how badly injured he could not say. Too, there were Apaches up there, and if one happened to be near the slide he would only have to step to the opening over Shell's head, sight and pull the trigger to end all of Morgan's worries. "Easy."

He slowly cleared a larger opening and then, bracing himself, used his hands and arms to drag his legs free. He paused, exhausted, to test his legs as well as he could. They were painful, but seemed unimpaired.

"So much for the easy part."

His hand groped downward through the rock and Shelter found his holster, the Colt remarkably still in it. Slowly, with great effort, he brought the Colt up beside his head.

"Now then." How would he handle this? Up and out as quickly as possible, or creep out like a snake from a squirrel's hole?

"Listen first," he said, and he found his brain was slowed by concussion. He had to stop, say it out loud, make sure his body understood the command before he proceeded. Too slow. Too slow to be an effective fighter.

"Take it slow then," he reminded himself. And he did.

Inch by inch he moved forward and upward, pausing to shove aside the heavier stones. And then with his Colt locked in his right hand he burst through, coming up into the empty night like a man rising from his grave.

He had the hammer on the Colt back, and his eyes stared out of a dust-streaked face, instantly alert, watching for the first thrust out of the darkness, for the savage attack of an Apache warrior.

But there was nothing. Nothing at all. The night was cold, the air fresh. The trail was empty. He dragged himself from the hole and sat on the rubble, his chest rising and falling sporadically, his head a whirling blur.

Nothing.

"Wake up, Morgan. Snap out of it!" he told himself silently. Because he saw no one, it didn't mean that there was no one there. That motivating notion finally sunk into Shell's consciousness and he scrambled from the slide to the deep shadows of the hollow behind it.

There he squatted on his haunches, listening, letting his head clear as he cleaned the Colt. It was so clogged with earth that he doubted it would have fired a few moments ago.

Snapping the gate shut he cocked it again. Then with the utmost caution he moved out, taking each step as if he walked on quicksand. Then he heard it.

A voice, a second, snarling word, and the faint creak of something far below. . . . He ran in a crouch to the edge of the rim and, flattening himself, peered down into the canyon.

Two horses lay dead there. The other two, still in harness stood up the canyon fifty feet or so. The coach, broken to kindling, scarcely recognizable, lay on its back against a massive water-polished boulder.

The moon clung to the western horizon, spreading a faint, diffused light—and by that light Shelter could see the Apaches.

Three of them. One held the horses. Squatting on his heels, rifle across his knees, he looked anxious. Two others were trying to rip open the warped, broken door of the stage. At their feet lay Ellie!

9

Ellie, surrounded by Apaches lay at the bottom of the night-shrouded gorge. Alive or dead? For a moment Shelter, lying flat at the rim of the canyon could not be sure, and then that small whimpering sound echoed thinly once more and he knew she was, temporarily, alive. Although, what her condition was he could not tell.

The Apaches argued briefly, in whispers. One wanted to get into the coach, the other argued that they should be going. Shelter caught only a word here and there.

"The woman . . . horses."

"More . . . you are too impatient . . . with the door."

"Crazy Kala! Look, ask . . ." He gestured toward the brave with the horses, but the first Apache was adamant. He wasn't about to leave any possible booty.

Shelter lost the rest of their conversation to the distance. He was no longer concentrating on that anyway. There was only one way to make sure Ellie did not fall into Apache hands. And despite what he had been reading lately in some of those progressive Eastern newspapers, it was truly a fate worse than death. He only wished some of those smart New Yorkers could see a woman who has been raped by every man in the tribe, who has had her face scarred by the Apache women, who has been driven from her mind and brutalized like an animal.

Shelter slid into a stony chute cut by runoff from the hills above, and he slipped down it toward the bottom of the gorge.

Once his boot dislodged a stone and he stopped, holding his breath. The Apaches seemed to fall silent, but after a while he heard their unconcerned voices. He continued on down.

Reaching the bottom of the canyon he was in complete darkness. The moon had faded and vanished below the empty horizon.

There was willow, dry and brown growing along the watercourse and Shell scrambled for that cover.

Then, moving like a cat through the shadows, he worked his way up the gorge. The voices of the Indians grew louder, although they spoke more quickly now and Shell could pick out only a handful of words.

"Camp . . . sunrise."

"No, not until . . ."

They were arguing among themselves and in a minute Shell could see why. The strongbox had been discovered and one wildly gesturing brave wanted to break into it. The others, apparently, were reluctant to do so. They kept mentioning a man named Tala, probably their lodge chief.

". . . to tell us . . ."

"Do what you will!"

The argument continued. Shelter had left the bottom of the wash and now he eased up into the rocks along the walls of the gorge. Fifty feet nearer and he would be in range. Twenty feet.

It was imperative that he draw near enough not to miss. The first shot an Apache fired could be into Ellie's head.

Then he was near enough, and an Apache's head came around, his open mouth soundless, his eyes narrowing. Shell saw his hand gesture sharply, silencing the others.

They had no reason to believe a man could be in those rocks. As far as they knew there was no living white in that gorge, and the Apache hadn't seen Shell—although the man was looking almost directly at him, that awareness was not reflected on his face.

But he had heard, or sensed, or smelled something, and to a man who survives by his senses, it was enough to bring instant caution.

He reached for his rifle which lay against the wheel of the coach and Shelter fired. The Apache was driven back, his arms flung wide as the rifle clattered free. Shelter wasted no time.

He switched his sights to the second Apache before the first had hit the ground, and he fired twice, saw the Apache slap at his eye and topple forward.

The third brave got to his pony's back and rode up the gorge, hidden by the horse and Shell, holding his breath, squeezed off a shot which caught the horse behind the shoulder and penetrated the heart.

The pony, a beautiful pinto buckled up and went down, rolling on its rider. The Apache's strangled scream filled the dark gorge for a brief, pitiful instant before it died away to a gurgling whine.

Shell leaped from the rocks, rushing across the rocky streambed, shoveling fresh loads into his Colt. There was no need to hurry. The Indian beneath the horse was dead. So were the others. All were young, not yet twenty; all were painted up for war. Two of them wore fresh scalps on their leggings. Now they would fight no more. They would walk the Apache sky trail. Now the night was still.

Except for the small, crumpled figure of a woman lying near the battered coach, and Shell rushed that way.

"Shelter," she said as if it hurt her throat to speak, and he knelt beside her, tenderly gathering her in his arms.

"Are you all right, girl? Are you all right?"

"I . . . Jesus I'm scared, look at me tremble. But I'm all right," she said with a weak smile. "I'll make it. But I don't care any more," she said, suddenly clamping her arms tightly around his neck. "I'm like Mel Giles—I don't care about this stinking stage line. No more!" She shook her head heavily. "I want to live. I want to hold you. Let the bastards have the gold, let them take whatever they want, but God, Shell, make them let me live!"

"You'll live, honey," he said softly. "I promise you that. It'll be all right."

But her tears were a hot flood against his face, and she trembled so violently that Shelter was not sure anything would ever again be all right in this woman's life.

"Up, baby," Shelter said, gripping her hands.

"I don't know if I can." Her voice had the tone of surrender in it.

"You've got to. The odds are these three young bucks were out prowling on their own, but if there are other Apaches up here you can bet they're hot-footing it in this direction."

"Oh!" she exclaimed and jumped to her feet. "When I saw them creeping down out of the rocks . . ." She shuddered.

"I know. I felt pretty much the same way," Shell said.

"What are you doing? Don't leave me, Shell!" He had turned and she grabbed his shirt. There was sheer terror in Ellie's eyes and he held her face between his hands, kissing her nose.

"I'm not leaving you, Ellie. I'm going to round up some horses. Then we're going to get off this mountain the quickest way possible."

He returned after a minute with the two Indian ponies. The third had died instantly when Shell's bullet entered its heart.

"Ugh," Ellie said, "they smell."

"Bear fat." Shell walked to the rear of the coach, Ellie's eyes following him intently.

"Now what?" she asked.

"This, of course." He hefted the strongbox,

finding it heavier than he remembered. The night's events had taken their toll.

"I don't care about that. Leave it."

"That doesn't make sense, Ellie. It's here, we're here. We'll take it into Troubadour with us."

"Troubadour," she agreed, "but no farther. I'm through with all of this and I mean it."

"Sure."

Shell fashioned a pack out of the harness that was left to him and slung the strongbox between the two remaining Tanner horses.

He helped Ellie onto the Indian pony's back and then swung up himself, happy to find that the Apache who had owned this horse used an American saddle with a blanket slung over it.

Then he led out, the two Tanner horses behind him, Ellie at his side.

They traveled down the long rocky gorge for nearly a mile, weaving through the brush and rocks before they found a way to return to the road.

Three hours later they were on the flats and when sunrise paled the desert skies they were within sight of Troubadour. Best of all there was smoke rising from the chimney of the house which was of stone, set on a low knoll.

"That's not war smoke," Shelter told the weary Ellie. "Somebody's up and cooking. I swear I can smell coffee and we must be a mile away."

Ellie didn't answer. By the morning sunlight Shell could see that her cheeks were badly scratched. There was a purple bruise on her forehead and a bit of scabbed blood below her ear.

Nevertheless she managed a smile when Jack

Upton came out of the stone house, rifle in his hand, peering into the sun. "Good God!" Upton said, and he came forward to help Ellie from her pony. "What happened, Miss Tanner?"

"Later, Jack," she said with an exhausted shake of her head. "Later, please."

"Sure." He was a lanky, long-jawed man in suspenders and a calico shirt. He glanced at Shelter and then slipped his arm around Ellie's waist, helping her to the house where a huge Indian woman in an apron stood watching from the porch.

"You know the Missus?" Upton asked.

"Yes, of course. How are you, Lupa?"

Lupa flushed with pleasure, happy that Ellie remembered her.

She was as wide as she was tall and cheerful. Shell took her for a Pima Indian. He never heard her say a word in English and doubted she knew any, but she could cook for Jack and she was good company for a lonely man in a lonely land.

During breakfast they told Upton everything that had happened and the long scowl on Jack's face deepened with each revelation. Finally he sighed, lit his cob pipe and said, "Well what are we going to do now?"

Shelter liked that. The man didn't fly into a panic or start worrying about where his next paycheck was going to come from. He was a steady, practical man and his first thoughts were on what should be done.

"You have a coach and team?" Shelter asked.

"Sure." Upton lifted a brushy eyebrow. "Why?"

118

"I'm going to finish the run," Shelter said.

"No, Shell!" Ellie said. She went white, the blood draining out of her face.

"Sure, Ellie. It's nothing to worry about. Look, we lost Guthrie a long ways back. That's not Apache country ahead, is it, Jack?"

"Not regular," Upton answered.

"But I told you, Shell," Ellie protested, "I don't care about the line anymore."

"Not right now you don't, and that's natural. You've had a rough time of it. But later you might care an awful lot."

"I won't," she said firmly.

"At least you'll have the option. Look, Ellie, what would Willie have done in this situation? You know damn well what he would have done. He signed a contract to make these gold deliveries to the Camby Mine Company, and by God, he would have done it. I mean to do the same. For Willie and for you."

"Want me to go?" Jack asked.

"No. Thanks, Jack, but I think you'd better stand tough here. The eastern leg is pretty well beat up. If we can at least count on you . . ."

"You can count on me," Upton said, rising to his full height, which was considerable. "They'll have to blast me out of here. And I'm not exactly alone. Lupa's got plenty of people up there in the hills."

Jack and Shelter went out together to harness the team. Ellie sat expressionlessly over her coffee, not looking up at them as they left.

"Must've been pretty rough," Upton said, his

capable fingers hitching the harness to a sleek bay. "I known that girl a long while, Morgan. She's always had plenty of spark. Now," he shook his head, "she looks beaten. I guess that's what they wanted," he said after a moment's thought.

Shelter and Upton loaded the strongbox and Lupa came from the house with some food wrapped in cheesecloth which Shelter accepted gratefully.

He stepped up into the box and Jack handed him the reins. Then, tugging down his hat against the fierce sun, he waited.

He didn't have to wait long. She emerged from the house looking weary but determined. She had pinned up her hair and she carried her shoulders squarely.

"Ready, boss?" Shell asked with a smile.

"I'm ready. I wish you'd just let me quit, Morgan, damn your blue eyes. But I'm ready. Hell, I'm a Tanner."

Jack Upton grinned and gave Ellie a hand up. The man and his wife stood watching as Shell urged the coach slowly forward and out of the yard.

After a mile Ellie could no longer stand it, "Shell, I'm sorry, but you'd better let me have those ribbons. You drive a stage like I drive nails, and believe me, that's not too damned well."

"You'll hurt my feelings," Shell said with mock seriousness.

She laughed, "That'll be the day, Shelter Morgan!"

Shelter shifted the reins to Ellie's hands. She

wanted to be on the near side so she lifted up and scooted over him. "There," she said, "just like coming home."

"A piece of cake from here," Shell said.

"Yeah." She smiled tightly. "I didn't want to do this you know. I really was ready to quit."

"Nobody forced you."

"No," she admitted. "But I watched you and Jack. Him not expecting any wages for his work, you caring about a dead company more than I did. Well, I started to feel a little ashamed."

"There was nothing to be ashamed of. Someone gets knocked down, he's not in a hurry to get back up, Ellie."

"Well, this is liable to be the last run anyway, isn't it? I mean, Dog Creek is closed, Gila Junction, probably Adobe Falls. We can't get passengers, drivers or guards."

"You've still got the Camby Mines contract."

"And we've still got the Guthries," she said, and there was an edge to her voice.

You do at that, Shell considered. For now. But he had his own ideas about the Guthries. He was damned if he'd let them take potshots at him any more. He was determined to find them and carry the war to the Guthries.

How many places could they be? They would have to stay clear of the Indians, yet remain near water. How many places out there on that desert would fit the bill?

He asked Ellie.

"I don't have to guess," she snapped. "Everyone knows where they are. Up on the Mesa Grande."

"But then . . . ?"

"Why don't the law chase them out? Good question, ask Snowden. He claims they can see him coming for miles and just take off. I don't know—if he's not involved in this, he's turning a blind eye to it."

"Mesa Grande." That stark jutting mesa not far from Crater. "You're sure?"

"Sure I'm sure. Poor Uncle Willie wanted to go after them once, but he couldn't raise a posse. Folks laughed, they wouldn't die for Tanner, they said. We didn't have enough men of our own. Shell!" Her eyes widened. "What are you thinking of?"

"Nothing," he said, patting her shoulder. "Nothing at all. Except Tucson." He grinned, hugged her, and kissed her neck.

"Hell," she said, blushing. "I don't know if I'd be much good at that—I'm stiff as a board from falling."

"I'm starting to get that way myself," he said with a grin, and she slapped his thigh playfully. "Giddy-up!" she shouted at the team, slapping the reins so that they cracked like a whip. "Me and my man got urgent business in Tucson."

Her hand rested on his thigh and after a minute it crept upward. "Stiff as a board, damned if it ain't," she laughed. "Get-up you lazy broomtails!"

Tucson was booming. Freight wagons and carriages jostled each other, the saloons rang out

122

with sounds of mischief and excitement. The Hotel Windsor, a three-story clapboard affair with gingerbread clinging like spider webs to the eaves, was newly opened and the yellow brick bank on the town square was going up rapidly. The sky was brilliant, the air torpid and dry between the rows of buildings.

The Camby Mine office was at the end of First Avenue.

Shelter swung down and went in, dusting his jeans, Ellie beside him.

"We'd like to see Mr. Camby," Ellie said to a dry, redheaded woman. "I'm Ellie Tanner."

After a minute the secretary returned from Camby's office. She nodded at the door and Ellie and Shelter went in. Camby, a thick-bodied, bespectacled man in a dark townsuit rose from behind his desk, his face a mask of astonishment.

"Miss Tanner?" he asked, peering at her with disbelief.

"I am," Ellie said. Camby darted a glance at Shelter.

"Sit down, please." Camby waved a hand in confusion. "I don't understand what . . ." Camby swallowed dryly. "Let me begin by asking, if I may, what are you doing here?"

"What we're doing here?" Ellie laughed. "We've brought your gold through to you, Mr. Camby."

"So!" He sagged into his chair, drawing a handkerchief from his pocket.

"What is it, Camby?" Shelter asked sharply.

"I was told . . . they said that Tanner had folded up. That another shipment had been lost."

"Who said?" Shelter demanded.

"The people from the Arizona Southern."

"The what?" Ellie asked.

"The . . . uh, other stage line."

Ellie came abruptly to her feet, her face taut, her eyes sparkling. "What other stage line? Since when has there been another stage line around here, and what did they want with you?"

"They wanted the contract, of course," Camby said, furiously patting his perspiring forehead with his handkerchief. "When they reported that you were out of business—your uncle dead."

"Wait a minute," Shell interrupted. "They knew Willie Tanner was dead?"

"Why, yes."

"And just how?" Shelter wondered, "could anyone but the Guthries know that?"

"There's some mistake here," Camby said miserably.

"You bet there is," Ellie said. "We've just come in with a shipment of gold. It's out front now. Now, if we're not working for you, Mr. Camby, does that mean that whatever's in that strongbox is ours and not yours?"

"No," he said, frantically. "Of course it's ours."

"Why? What gives you the right to claim that gold?" Ellie persisted. Shell was proud of her; Camby was jolted.

"Why—we had a contract, Miss Tanner," he said pleadingly.

"You're damn right." Ellie tossed her head. "We had a contract. Do you want me to read it to you, Mr. Camby? Tanner has sole and exclusive rights to transport Camby Mines payroll shipments. So long as we are physically able to perform that service."

"Yes, but that is just the point, Miss Tanner. These people from Arizona Southern arrived yesterday and informed me that you had gone out of business. They had quite an impressive party—a coach and ten outriders, hard-looking men. We talked about security and schedules and . . . well, I gave them the Camby contract."

"But you can't do that!" Ellie's small fist banged down on the mine boss's desk, startling him. "I'll sue."

"Miss Tanner—there's no need for that, I assure you. I was only trying to solve the company's problem. I was sorry, of course, to hear that your uncle had been killed, that the line was shut down, but I gave it full credence, mistakenly, it seems, and then hired a new company—it was only business.

"Now that I know you are still working, the contract is yours. Unless of course," and here Camby's smile altered slightly, "you default on another shipment. In Paragraph Four of our agreement—"

"I am well aware of what Paragraph Four stipulates, Mr. Camby."

Simply, the paragraph gave Tanner a margin for error, the circumstances in the territory being fully considered, but the loss of three shipments was grounds for terminating the agreement. Was there any way in hell Ellie could guarantee another gold shipment would not be lost?

Still she held her head up. She demanded and received payment for the gold after it was lugged into Camby's office and gone over by the mine boss and a small man in pince-nez glasses. Once, absently, Camby put his hand down on the lid of the box and pulled it away, wiping off the rust brown, crusty substance which clung to his palm. Shelter didn't think there was any point in telling him it was an Apache's blood.

"Can you beat that!" Ellie said as they walked out into the sunlight and dry heat of Tucson. "Somebody horning in on Tanner."

"I don't think it's just good timing, either," Shell commented.

"No?" They stepped down into the dusty street, let a yahooing cowboy ride past, waving a bottle and a gun, and turned toward the hotel.

"I think it was planned all along, Ellie. I think all of the trouble Tanner has had was designed to drive you out of business. The Camby Mine contract is a rich one. Tanner was doing well and someone got envious. Now," he said, "it looks like they've figured it's time to move in and grab the spoils."

"You mean . . ." She stopped in the middle of the street. "Someone hired the Guthries to drive us out of business?"

"Sure. What profit is there in burning down stage stations, killing horses, destroying coaches? None at all for your hold-up artist."

"But for someone who wanted to cripple Tanner Line and take over the route, the passenger trade, the mine shipments . . ."

"Sure. It was either that or compete honestly. And Tanner already had the Camby contract sewn up. Answer—crush Tanner."

They stepped onto the porch of the hotel, standing for a moment in the dry shade cast by the awning. "Then who?" Ellie asked, shaking her head.

"Simple. Find out who Arizona Southern is, and you'll know. Proving it—now, that's something else again."

"And that puts us right back where we started, doesn't it?" Ellie was deflated. "I mean, even if we knew it was the mayor of Tucson, we couldn't prove it, could we? He could just say he saw Tanner was faltering and stepped in?"

"Exactly. But don't worry about that. We'll get proof."

"We will?" She glanced dubiously at him as they strolled into the carpeted hotel lobby.

"Yes. Or I will. You shall run Tanner for a time. But," Morgan said in a whisper as they approached the desk, "I don't think it is the mayor of Tucson who's responsible, so don't start any vicious rumors."

Ellie giggled and the desk clerk frowned.

"Have you got two rooms side by side?" Shelter asked. The man nodded, turning the register so that Shell and Ellie Tanner could sign in.

"Who, then Shell? Who is Arizona Southern?"

"We'll have another talk with Camby. He'll tell us what he knows. They must have left a name, even if it's a phony, and an address. And I'll give you good odds that the address is Crater, Arizona."

127

10

The Chinese kid came and left, filling the wooden tub with hot water. Shelter eased into the tub, his muscles sore; gradually the water loosened the tense muscles.

The door between the adjoining rooms was open and Ellie called, "I'm so stiff I can hardly get in!"

"Need help?"

"Later."

The steam rose up around Shelter's ears. His body went limp in the scalding water—or most of it did.

He had eaten his fill of roast beef, potatoes and gravy, corn on the cob, fresh local plums, and apple pie. Then he had had three dark cups of coffee, watching as Ellie stuffed herself, relishing each bite, nearly matching Shell's intake.

Then Shelter had smoked a rare cigar and helped himself to hotel whiskey, settling into a hazy lethargy while Ellie nodded sleepily across the table.

"Let's call for baths," Shell said suddenly and

Ellie had purred a response.

Shell went down and had the management haul two tubs up. Then there was a procession of small Chinese men carrying hot water from the kitchen until the wooden tubs were brim-full.

He sat there now dozing, amazed at how far away and of how little concern Arizona Southern, Guthrie, and even Du Rose himself were.

The body was satisfied. Filled, warmed, relaxed. And the rest of the world seemed far away. Shell heard a footstep and looked up.

Ellie, naked and glistening with water, walked into the room through the connecting door. She held her arms out from her body. Her legs, beautiful and silky as they were, moved like wooden pegs. She looked miserably at Shell.

"I thought that water would soak all the stiffness out."

"Didn't work?"

"No, dammit. It's worse if anything. I couldn't recommend riding a stage down a five-hundred foot slope."

"Let me see."

She came to him and he turned her, finding the purple bruise which stained her lovely white hip. He leaned his head to her and kissed it.

"That seems to help a little," she murmured. She turned, smiling as if it hurt her mouth when she did so. Looking down at him in the tub Ellie said, "My God, are you human, Mr. Morgan!"

"Very." He looked at her again. "Poor Ellie," he said, and poor she was just then. Her back was scraped, her leg discolored with bruises. A knot was appearing on her forehead. "At least no vital parts were damaged."

"Just my brain, apparently," she said, sitting on the edge of the tub, dangling a hand in the water. A hand which slowly, of its own volition, swam to where Shelter's erection bobbed above the soapy water.

Her full, pendulous breasts dangled tantalizingly, glossed by the dim lamplight in Shelter's room and her hand closed swiftly around his cock. "Come on, Morgan, you've soaked enough."

"Haven't got the stiffness out yet."

"I know."

Slowly he stood, and Ellie kept hold of him as if afraid of losing him. "Door in your room locked?"

"Of course, darling. I've been planning this since we checked in."

"Think you can handle it?"

"Stiff as I am, sore as I am, I won't notice it in five minutes," she believed. "Not if it's you taking care of me, Mr. Morgan."

"Why all the 'Mr. Morgan' tonight?"

"Because," she said, kissing his damp, naked chest, "I feel very formal. This is a formal occasion. I came dressed for a very formal ceremony."

"Ah, now that you've explained it—Miss Tanner."

She had gotten a towel and she knelt before him, drying him carefully, working upward from his feet, dabbing diligently at his crotch, turning him to buff his buttocks which earned themselves a light kiss.

Then Ellie stood. She began drying his chest, stopped, threw the towel aside and said, her voice breathy, "Enough, enough. I'm only flesh and blood, you know."

"Good thing." Shell wrapped his arms around her, their naked abdomens pressing together, their mouths joined in a deep kiss.

"Oh!" Ellie cried out and stepped back, still holding her arms stiffly away from her body. "Pain," she laughed, "pain!"

"Maybe we'd better forget it."

"No chance, Mr. Morgan. I've been thinking about this since Troubadour."

"Lie down on the bed," Shell told her. He even helped her walk that way, his hand on her full, swaying rear. "Not like that, on your stomach," he said.

"If you say so," she said doubtfully. She turned like a scarecrow in the wind and flopped face downward onto the bed.

Shell scooped up her legs and placed them on the bed. "Now then," he said. Easing up, he straddled her, massaging her shoulders with long sensuous strokes of his fingers, working the soreness out of her shoulders.

Ellie murmured comfortable sounds and luxuriated in the sensations. She was drifting through a twilight world, feeling his strong, gentle hands work across her shoulders, down her back, bringing comfort wherever they touched her. She shivered as one of his intermittent kisses touched the small of her back, near the tail of her spine, then smiled more deeply as she felt him pressed against her buttocks, felt the throb, the heat of him.

"That," she demanded as a child might. Her hand stretched downward, searching for Shell's crotch.

"You sure?"

"That, that," she said drowsily and Shelter complied. He lifted her hips slightly and placed a pillow beneath her stomach.

Then he approached her slowly, liking the gentle silkiness of her flesh, the pale glistening of her as his fingers slowly traced patterns across her. He spread her like a pale pink rose to his delighted eye and eager fingers, as Ellie, breathing more rapidly, sank into sweet sensuality.

"Hell of a thing, having to do everything myself," Shell complained teasingly. Ellie only purred. He eased himself into position, placing the head of his shaft against her soft, dewy flesh, watching her quiver, open to accept him. He sat like that a minute, on his knees, Ellie's legs spread, her hips raised by the pillow, and then he slowly eased forward, watching as the head of his manhood disappeared into her awaiting flesh.

Ellie gasped, and looking at her face he saw that her mouth was open, her eyes half-closed. Her dark hair was spread across the pillow, her fists clenched, and as Shelter slid forward another inch her body began to quiver anew and she beat her fists against the mattress.

"More, more, Morgan. Drive it in me. Please. More, more, more." And Shell obliged the lady, wedging his shaft into her, feeling the silky expansion of the soft sheath of flesh which was Ellie Tanner.

Her hips began to move, although it was painful. She whimpered with each effort. Shell worked his way forward until he was buried in her, until he could feel her throbbing along his entire length, feel her flooding with dew.

"God, oh my. Please . . ." She murmured strings of meaningless words and Shelter began slowly to sway against her, his hands on her full white ass. Slowly he worked into her and then out, moving in small circles, his hand kneading Ellie's buttocks. His own loins began to throb, to demand release as he thrust against her, lifting her higher and higher. She continued to mumble pleasurable words and she pounded her fist against the pillow, gasping as Shelter drove it home time and again, flooding her head with brilliant images, her womb with a surging, swelling warmth which built to a flood.

Her ears rang, her pulse raced through her skull. Electric flashes rose from her abdomen to her nipples, fanned out across her body and there was a sweet rising tension which felt so completely wonderful that she could not stand it. She wanted him to stop, to split her in two, to bite her until he tore her flesh.

A rush of color, of sound, of sensation swept over Ellie, drowning her consciousness, becoming the only thing that mattered in this world, and she collapsed feeling everything go liquid, warm, velvet.

Shelter saw the tight smile on her face, saw the

relaxed loll of her head, the unclenching of her hands. He watched as he entered her, stroking against her, watched the ripe flare of her buttocks, the sweep of her spine, the soft white shoulders, the full breast beneath her. And he felt a sudden undeniable surge of raw need rising.

He clawed at her, needing her then, and he let himself go, feeling the shocking drain of a delicious climax, feeling the last surge of wild fulfillment and the slow ebbing throb of his body as he finished, holding perfectly still, positioned deep within the lush body of Ellie Tanner.

"How's the pain?" he asked after a while.

"Pain, what pain?"

He lay beside her then and she draped a thigh across his. A languid, comforting breast offered itself to his mouth and he kissed it gently. After a time Shelter realized he was cool, realized that he had somehow fallen asleep. He started to apologize to Ellie, then saw that she too was in a deep, exhausted, satisfied sleep. And he smiled.

Rising, he turned the lamp low and watched her as she slept for long hours. He thought of her funny, puckered smile, of her clever sense of humor, of her determination—and he thought of the men out there who wanted to kill her.

They didn't know Ellie Tanner. They didn't know that she was a living, vivacious creature, full of honey and milk, bright and outgoing, loyal and quite courageous. To them she was an object in the way of profit. Something to be disposed of, to be rolled off the trail.

And slowly an anger built in Morgan. They had

killed her old uncle and they would kill her. She wasn't strong enough to stop them and the law wouldn't take a hand.

That only left him. Shell rose and walked to the window, watching the few people on the streets of Tucson at this late hour.

Ellie snored briefly, and Shelter smiled, turning from the window. He himself was suddenly not sleepy. He had certain plans to be worked out in his mind, matters which took serious consideration.

He sat down at the small writing desk in the corner of the hotel room and while Ellie slept away her exhaustion he placed his Colt revolver on that desk and disassembled it, carefully cleaning and oiling every part.

He woke her with a kiss and a cup of coffee, and she sat up, her eyes sparkling, her dark hair tousled, looking fat and satisfied.

"I could get spoiled real quick," she said, sipping her coffee.

"I think you already are, child," Shell said, sitting on the bed beside her. "How do you feel?"

"Terrific," she said silkily.

"I mean the soreness and all," Shell smiled, kissing her ear. "Can you travel?"

"Travel?" her eyes narrowed. "I suppose, sure—but why? What's the hurry, Shelter. We haven't got anything urgent to do, nothing that couldn't wait a day or two. No sense in trying to keep to a schedule when we've got no passengers, no cargo, no stations, no nothing."

"No," he agreed, "I'm not worried about the schedule. But we do have business to attend to. At least I do. Pressing business, Ellie. And the sooner it's cleaned up the better."

He watched her as she dressed, an occupation he found so pleasurable that he felt inclined to reverse the process.

"I went to see Camby again," Shelter told her.

"What? When? How long did I sleep, Shelter?"

"It's nearly noon."

"I'm a fine one," she said, struggling to lift her sore arms to wriggle into her shirt. Shell rose and helped her.

"Let's get you in a dress some time."

"Let's get me out of one." She kissed his chin.

"That too."

"So, what did Camby say?"

Nothing much useful, Shelter had to tell her. "The man he talked to was tall, fairly tall, dark brown hair, or blond. He was covering up, but what could I do?"

"I would have slapped him," Ellie said fiercely.

"Thought about it myself, but I didn't have a yen to see the Tucson jail firsthand."

"How about an address—he must have had one, and he couldn't lie about it, could he?" Ellie tucked her hair into her hat.

"No, he showed it to me."

"Interesting?"

"Not exactly: 'Southern Arizona Stage Company, care of General Delivery, Crater, Arizona.'"

"Informative."

"It might be. If the postal clerk's got a decent memory."

"I'll bet he doesn't. I'll bet he was tipped an eagle not to have."

"Then a double-eagle might do wonders," Shell said.

"Tanner Line money, you free-spender?"

"Naturally."

They spent a few more hours in Tucson, talking to the end-of-line agent, Mike Torres who was sleepy-eyed but sharp as a tack. He was paid for the next two months and given cash to purchase feed for the horses. Tanner credit was no longer much good in Tucson.

Then, stocking up the coach with flour, sugar, coffee, and beans for Jack Upton at Troubadour, they headed east with a new team. Ellie had posted notices offering "secure positions" with Tanner lines around town, but she didn't expect a rush of response.

They rolled through to Troubadour without incident, with Ellie in a silent mood and Shelter doing his own quiet thinking.

Jack Upton was paid as well, and he seemed surprised. Ellie had also collected a few odds and ends of yardage for Lupa in Tucson, predominately bright yellow and red cotton fabric which delighted Jack's Indian wife.

"A lot of good will for a few dollars," Ellie said as they rolled out again with a fresh team, but Shelter knew there was more to it than that.

It was a lonesome life out there, and it was a life that Ellie had led for a long while herself. She knew how a small gift could brighten the dull sameness of days on the desert.

"What now?" Ellie asked as they swept north of the mountains toward Adobe Falls Station and home.

"Let's have a look at Adobe Falls, see what's left. Then the both of us had better drive into Crater. See if you can find some sort of temporary office and rebuild the line from there. You can't stay out here."

"No," Ellie agreed. Her confidence was beginning to falter and it collapsed completely when they reached Adobe Falls.

Burned to the ground—the blacksmith's shop, the drivers' bunkhouse, the main house which had been home. She drew up the team and sat staring, hollow-eyed at what had been home.

"I suppose it will still work." Her eyes shifted to the fresh graves among the sycamores. But—Shell knew what she was thinking—did she care any more? Care enough to keep on fighting, to watch more men die.

"I'll straighten this out, Ellie," he said softly. "I promise you that. I'll straighten it out, or—"

"Or die?" Her face was panic-stricken. "Shelter, I can't see another man die. And especially not you. For what? A few dollars a year!" She laughed.

"Because you're right, Ellie," he told her. "Because you have the right to make a living without these vultures tearing you down."

"I don't care if I'm right, if you die!" she said sharply.

"I'm not going to die, don't you worry," Shell

said, but she seemed not to hear him.

"I suppose if I can find an office in Crater I can put the drivers up in the hotel until Adobe Falls can be rebuilt. Why, there must be plenty of teamsters who'd take a stagecoach job." Her eyes were distant, determined, and Shelter knew that she was after all a Tanner, that she would stick.

"Let's get on in," she said, and she shook her head with determination. Ellie turned the coach and they rolled toward Crater. The massive bulk of Mesa Grande stood starkly against the desert, drawing Shelter's eyes. There, he thought, there is the key, the way to end all of this.

It was late afternoon, a bright sun glaring down on the empty streets of Crater, when the Tanner Line coach with Ellie at the reins rolled up the main street and headed for the stables on Front.

There the hostler unhitched the team and rubbed them down without asking any questions, a point which Ellie seemed to appreciate.

"I'm tired," she said, and she was obviously beat. Dust clung to her clothes and face; her eyes were red and weary. "How about dinner at the hotel, and a nice bath."

"Sounds great." Shell kissed her salt-tasting forehead. "Why don't you do just that."

She pulled away, glancing up at him. "I meant the two of us, Shelter."

"I know you did. I've a few things to do."

"You can't be going to the Mesa Grande."

"Not right now."

"But you mean to!" She grabbed his arms and clung to him. "It's foolish; it's not worth it."

"Foolish it may be. We'll have to see if it's worth it. I'm going, Ellie," he said and she knew he would no matter what she said or did.

She dropped her hands, exasperation and weariness in her eyes. "I need a bath."

"Take one for me," Shell said lightly. And then he was gone, leading the leggy gray gelding he had rented from the stable. Up Main Street he went, a tall, determined man with a low-slung Colt and murder in his eyes. Ellie turned toward the hotel, determined not to think about it any longer.

The post office was in the general store. Behind a wire cage an aproned clerk finished sorting the letters into the wooden pigeon holes and glanced up.

"Yes, sir."

Shell slapped a gold double-eagle down on the counter before he said anything and the man's eyes lighted.

"Yes, sir!" he said with excessive joviality.

"I have a question for you," Morgan said, leaning his elbows on the counter. "I want to know who picks up the mail for the Arizona Southern stage line."

"The what?" the clerk asked. He looked at the twenty dollar gold piece, his eyes bright and then shook his head, eyeing the tall dark man who stood before him.

"Arizona Southern," Shell repeated.

"Got me. I never notice those things," the man shrugged.

"I think you do," Shelter said mildly. Then, in a smooth, easy motion he laid his Colt on the counter where the double eagle glittered. The clerk's eyes narrowed and his mouth fell open a few inches.

"What is this?" the clerk asked, licking his lips. He glanced around the store, finding it empty except for old Mrs. Jacklin who was sorting through the lace remnants.

"This is called choosing your poison," Shelter said so softly that the clerk had to tilt his head forward and listen intently. He didn't like the hard, frosty look in the tall man's eyes, the nerveless tone of his voice. He especially didn't like the black, unblinking eye of that big Colt .44 muzzle.

"I don't get you," he stammered.

"I think you do." Shell lounged on the counter, both elbows on the scarred wood, his hat tilted forward. "It's simple. Two items." He rested a hand on the Colt. "A .44 revolver and a twenty dollar gold piece. All you have to do is choose one or the other."

"Look mister—" The man's lips were white, compressed.

"The Colt, did you say?" Shelter asked and he picked it up.

"Bert Quail," the clerk blurted out. Then he stepped back, his body rigid. "Quail's the one."

"Thanks." Shelter turned, holstered the Colt and walked out.

Light was falling to dusk outside as Shelter stepped into the saddle of the rented gray. Bert Quail—well, it wasn't much of a surprise really. It had to be someone with the power to keep the law

141

from interfering, someone who had the assets to build his own stage line. Quail fit both of those requirements.

Shell had known it all along somehow, or suspected it at least. The fury in Bert Quail as he tried to throw Morgan out of Phoebe Strawn's office. Awfully damned jealous for a man who had just met the lady.

Unless his motive wasn't jealousy but hatred of Morgan, or fear of him. And why would that be? At that time Shell hadn't yet signed on with Tanner Lines. Interesting, Shelter thought, as he turned the gray out onto the wide desert toward the hulking mass of the Mesa Grande.

11

The horse's hoofs made muted whooshing sounds as it walked across the sandy floor of the great basin. Above the stars, large and blue, sparkled in a black sky.

The lights of Crater twinkled across the distance, red and yellow, small and futile. Ocotillo cactus waved long, narrow. arms of warning as Shelter neared the square topped, massive Mesa Grande. He rode loosely now, knowing he was in outlaw territory, knowing these men needed no excuse to cut him down, to leave him for buzzard bait.

As he neared the mesa he found himself riding through head-high willow brush watered by the runoff from the fluted red flanks of the great landform. Cicadas hummed against the warm night, falling silent briefly as Shelter passed.

The nearer he approached, the more impossible it all seemed. To climb that mesa in the dark took more skill as a climber than he possessed, and indeed he had no ropes or other equipment.

By starlight he could see one zigzagging trail up

toward caprock, but this undoubtedly would be guarded. He had only one hole card to work with and he decided to play it and see how the chips fell.

It was another half-hour before he reached the foot of the mesa which now thrust magnificent shoulders against the sky, blacking out half of the stars above.

Morgan found the foot of the trail, loosened his pistol in his holster and started on up, expecting anything.

The trail wound higher, switching back as it climbed above the black, smooth desert below. Here and there stunted cedar clung tenaciously to the red rock, and Shell saw one massive bristlecone pine tilted crazily out over a massive ravine.

There was no point in stealth now. Once he was on the caprock trail he would be spotted, so he tilted back his hat and began whistling, walking the gray up the water-rutted trail.

He was briefly among flowering manzanita brush, shoulder-high to the horse, as the trail dipped down and then rose sharply toward the heights.

The voice was sudden and harsh: "Hold it right there or get shot out of the saddle."

"All right. Don't get trigger-happy." Shell reined up and peered toward the darkness, seeing no one. "Who's out there?"

"Never mind who I am. Who the hell are you?"

The voice was nearer now and Shelter heard the sound of gravel crunching beneath a boot. He kept his hands high, his face and voice bland.

"I got a message from Bert Quail. Are you Guthrie?"

"No, I ain't Guthrie," the man snarled. "You say you got a message? Give it to me."

"Can't. Quail says to give it straight to Guthrie."

"I suppose that means I got to take you all the way up," the guard grumbled. Now he was out of the shadows and Shell could see a tall, hatchet-faced man wearing a torn leather jacket. He carried a Winchester in his hands.

He asked Shelter, "What's happening? More trouble?"

"I think it's all over," Shelter said with a smile. "When that Tanner brat got to Tucson and Camby gave her the sad news, she just folded up. Sat in his office and cried."

"I always knew she'd give up," the guard said. "What else could she do?"

"Nothin' much." The guard was just beside Shell's horse now, his face relaxed but still wary. He tried to identify Shelter, but could not. Shell only hoped the outlaw hadn't spent that much time in Crater, enough to know that Shell wasn't one of the locals. It was a gamble, but so far he hadn't been shot. Shell's easy chatter about Ellie Tanner seemed to have relaxed the guard. After all, how could anyone but a Quail man know about it?

"If that's the message I'll give it to the old man," the guard offered in what was nearly a friendly tone.

"There's more, but it's something to do with the

pay-off, and I was told just to give the message to Guthrie myself."

"Suits me," the guard shrugged. "All over but the shouting then, is it?"

"Looks like it," Shell agreed. He frowned. "Damned horse must've picked up a rock. Mind if I get down?" He did before the guard could argue. "He's been walking stiff-legged."

"I've had enough of this country anyway," the guard said. "I'm going to pocket my pay and head back for Texas."

"Hear about Reyes?" Shell asked, lifting the gray's right hind hoof for inspection. The guard peered at the hoof as well.

"No."

"He's out of it," Shell said, glancing up, shaking his head slightly. "Dead."

"I figured as much," the guard said.

"I'll be damned," Shell muttered. "What do you make of this?"

The guard bent lower over the hoof as Shell pointed with his index finger. He bent a little lower. "I don't see nothin'."

And then he saw nothing for a long while. Shelter brought his right hand around with all of his weight behind it. It was a letter-perfect hook which caught the guard on the shelf of the jaw and dropped him soundlessly to the earth where he lay, mouth open, sleeping soundly.

Shelter looked up the trail and dragged him into the brush where he stripped off the guard's belt and lashed his hands and ankles together, gagging him by balling up his scarf and stuffing it into his mouth.

Then, working quickly, Shell shouldered into the guard's leather jacket and picked up his torn gray stetson. Walking up the ravine a way, he stopped, listening to the darkness. After a minute he heard a horse shift its feet, heard the faint munching sounds of an animal chewing foliage.

Walking that way fifty feet he found the outlaw's black horse and the man's bedroll. A cold fire rested in the center of the roughly cleared camp. The perimeter of the clearing was littered with old cans and bottles.

Shelter went to the horse, gathered the reins, and led it back down the ravine, past the still-sleeping guard. Then, switching his saddle to the outlaw's black, he turned the gray free to make its way back to the stable in Crater.

Shelter stepped into leather, carrying his rifle across the saddlebows. Hat tipped low over his eyes, he began his ride to the high mesa.

He hadn't gone a half mile when a voice greeted him from out of the brush.

"What's the matter, Bob?"

Shelter grunted a reply, waved a hand and rode on.

"Bob?" the voice called again, but Shelter didn't even slow down. He was riding now up a wedge-shaped cut in the caprock where pine grew to fifty feet and more. There was the pleasant, soft sound of a brook gurgling past, and ahead the soft, hazy glow of a campfire.

Just how in hell he was ever going to get off of the mesa, he hadn't figured. There would be

147

trouble, he knew that—it was what he had come for, and there would be no sneaking away. Even now, he thought glumly, the second sentry might be having thoughts about why "Bob" had left his post. He might decide to ride up and find out.

Even without that to worry about, Shelter knew he was in for it. A single man riding into an armed outlaw camp. If you thought about it, it sounded suicidal, or plain stupid. He tried not to think about it. He had made his share of night raids during the war, and some after. He had learned that the darkness can be a formidable ally—or a deadly enemy.

The fire showed bright red against the meadow below now. Shelter steered the black into the tall timber and circled slowly toward it. Beyond the meadow was more timber and then what must have been three square miles of nearly barren, flat caprock.

He slipped from the horse's back a hundred yards from the fire, ground tethering the animal. Then, with a look down the backtrail which told him nothing in this darkness, he stepped and slid down the slope before him, eyes on the fire and the dark figures of the men surrounding it.

One man played a muted mouth harp and soft laughter came from the other side of the camp. The fire glowed pleasantly.

The camp was like that of a weary crew of cowboys. There was the smell of coffee, the lingering scent of tobacco. Men spoke together quietly. Like this, it was difficult to hate them, to think of killing them.

Yet these were the same men who had killed Mel Giles, killed the old man and his wife at Gila Junction, killed Willie Tanner. Cutthroats who only resembled human beings in the darkness, in the soft glow of the fire. They spoke like men, moved like men, but it was all illusion—they were rabid animals, a pack of renegade wolves which needed to be put down before they killed again.

Shell slipped through the night shadowed trees, the star-crossed shadows webbing the blanket of pine needles underfoot.

He moved silently toward the camp, watching the fire light the shadows. Mentally he counted them, constantly measuring and reevaluating his chances. They weren't getting any better.

Guthrie had a dozen men in camp, and probably half that many elsewhere as sentries. Shell was near enough to the camp to see the scar on the cheek of one lean-jawed man when he pressed himself flat against the earth and listened, his eyes searching the firecast shadows.

There! It was Guthrie. He knew him from his description and by the way he lorded it over the other men. Bald, hulking, nearly toothless, he was dressed in a checked red flannel shirt, his small sullen eyes glaring at the man across the fire from him.

And that man—jackpot! Shelter's heart lifted into his throat—that man was beyond doubt Charles Du Rose. Shell's brain hammered with the surge of blood.

All he had to do was lift his Colt, sight down that smooth blue barrel and squeeze off. And then what? They would kill him, of course, and Guthrie would proceed to drive Ellie Tanner into the ground.

It was with strange exhilaration that Shelter lay there, the scent of pine in his nostrils, the palest light of the rising moon in his eyes, watching Du Rose and Guthrie. Two butchers and he had them. Had them . . . yet some animal plea had lodged itself in the back of his mind. The plea for survival.

And so he did not walk forward, his Colt banging away in the night, shooting down Guthrie and Du Rose as he himself was shot to bloody doll rags.

He pressed himself closer to the damp earth, trying to figure a way, to put a handle on this problem. How much time was there? Very little probably. The guards would be changed and someone would find Bob asleep or struggling angrily with his bonds and send up the alarm. How? His brain writhed with the problem. How to snare Du Rose and Guthrie, and stay alive himself.

And then Du Rose presented an answer.

Shelter saw him rise from the skinned log where he sat and at first Shelter thought unreasonably that Du Rose had spotted him.

But the dark-faced man, hatless and swaggering, walked to where Guthrie rested and said, "We've got to talk, Jeremiah."

"We've talked before—too damned much," the outlaw growled, his hat tipped down over his face.

"I agree. So let's settle it now. It's nearly over,

and you and I both know it. The girl can't hold out."

"I told you once, I want to be paid off like we agreed," Guthrie said with lazy arrogance. "Anything else you got to say on that subject, I don't want to hear it."

The men around the fire, Guthrie's men, were listening. And Du Rose, in obvious irritation said, "Not here, Guthrie. Let's take a walk."

"And what's in it for me if I do walk?"

"Money. Gold money," Du Rose said quietly. "And that's all any of us are in this for, isn't it?"

"What are you offering?"

"Take a walk, I'll tell you," Du Rose said. Guthrie, slowly, cautiously, stood. He hefted the Winchester which rested beside him.

"You don't mind if I carry my rifle along, do you?" he asked.

"Carry a cannon if you want," Du Rose said impatiently.

"That might not be enough with you," Guthrie said wryly.

"If you don't like it . . ."

"I don't, but it doesn't matter. As long as we all get paid."

"Oh, we'll get paid," Du Rose said, his voice suddenly silky. "Come on." He nodded his head. "Too many ears around here."

Together the two men walked away from the firelit camp. Guthrie, Shell noticed with grudging admiration, was careful to let Du Rose walk in front of him.

Shell worked his way upslope for a ways and

then circled the hill, following Du Rose and Guthrie at a distance. The two men walked a hundred yards from the camp before they stopped. Even then Du Rose was cautious, speaking in low tones so that Shelter had to creep closer, crawling over the cool earth to hear them.

"What is all this now?" Guthrie asked.

"It's about our cut."

"What about it? It suits me."

"Does it?" Du Rose's voice was wheedling. "Hell, Guthrie, who did all the work running this job? You. Who lost a son, you or that damned Quail?"

"It was his job. We hired on for wages. As for my boy, well—I'll find that son of a bitch Morgan and kill him if it's the last thing I do."

"I know you will." Du Rose leaned up against the massive, wood-pecker pocked trunk of a jackpine. The pale moonlight turned his face to wax. "But what I'm talking about is just compensation."

"What d'you mean?" Guthrie asked suspiciously.

"I'm talking about Quail's share."

"Hell," Guthrie shrugged, "it was his money. We only supplied the muscle."

"And now he's going to profit from it. Profit big once he gets that stage line running."

"So?" asked Guthrie with suspicion.

"So—why shouldn't we have a little more now? Say double what he's offered."

"He won't stand still for it."

"He will if we threaten to give him exactly what Tanner got," Du Rose said with a slow serpentine smile.

Guthrie stood silently in the shadows of the pines, his face expressionless for a time as Shelter watched. It had all become quite clear now. Du Rose had told Quail that a man called Morgan might be looking for him. That explained Quail's flare-up over what was a minor incident with Phoebe Strawn.

Quail was a man who wanted to run a stage line, and damn the outfit that was already working. He had hired Guthrie, possibly through Du Rose, to drive the Tanner Line out of business. That accomplished, Quail stood to rake in big profits from the Camby Mines contract. It was no risk for Quail at all—he knew in advance that the outlaws wouldn't be hitting *him*.

Slowly the idea spread through Jeremiah Guthrie's brain and a deep toothless smile developed. "That's blackmail, Du Rose," he said.

"Yes," Du Rose said, his voice flat, "I guess that's what they call it. Who are we in this for, Jeremiah? For Quail or for ourselves? We got the man on the ropes every bit as much as we had Tanner there. He pays a little more or he gets the same trouble Tanner got."

"It stinks," Guthrie said.

"Sure it does. Like what we did to Willie Tanner. But it pays, Jeremiah. It pays. What do you say?"

"You'll talk to him?"

"I will. I'll lay it out nice and plain for old Bert."

"All I got to do is stay put?" Guthrie asked uncertainly.

"That's all. You know he won't buck us. He can't. He can't call in the law because of what we know. He can't fight us because he can't get the people to buck Jeremiah Guthrie. It can't fail."

"Seems I've heard that before from you. In El Paso."

"One bad turn out of how many? Come on, Jeremiah. Old Du Rose won't let you down."

"Unless you see a chance to cut my throat too."

"Partner!" Du Rose said with indignation, but Guthrie wasn't taken in by the histrionics. He knew Du Rose too well, apparently.

"All of that don't matter," Guthrie said after a while. "I don't see what I've got to lose. All right," he nodded, "you offer it up to Quail, see how he takes it."

"I know how he'll take it," Du Rose laughed. "He'll be mad as hell, but what else can he do except pay?"

"When you plan on seeing him?" Guthrie inquired.

"Tonight. Why wait? The sooner the better."

"All right. I'm with you." Then to Shell's surprise, the somber Guthrie broke out in a hoarse chuckle. His voice was startlingly malevolent now that he had decided to throw in with Du Rose. "This'll teach that towny a thing or two." He laughed again.

Shell felt like joining them. He felt a pleasure as deep and as devious as Guthrie's flooding him. He knew exactly where he could find Du Rose this evening, and to get at him he wouldn't have to fight his way through half of Guthrie's outlaws.

He could take Du Rose and use him against Quail. In their scurry to avoid prosecution, they would likely implicate each other. Guthrie could wait until later. He was only a hired thug.

Shell waited until Guthrie and Du Rose had gone before he circled soundlessly up the hill, finding the glistening black horse in the moonlight.

Then he saddled and, veering far from the camp, made his way back toward the rim trail. If Bob was still where Shelter had left him, then Shelter had safe passage down.

Of course if they had found him trussed and gagged—well it had been a damned good try in that case.

His luck was with him. Passing the first checkpoint he heard a low whistle which he returned with a wave. Then, holding his breath against the impact of molten, tumbling lead, he rode past.

But there was no following shot and Shell's heart began to slow. Bob was still tied, but no longer unconscious. He was writhing like a bobcat in a rain barrel and just as mad.

"Calm down," Shelter told him as he stood over the outlaw, pistol to his head. "You and me are going for a ride. Alive or dead, Bob, it's your choice."

Funny how that seemed to calm Bob. His eyes were wide and white in the glare of the moon as

Shell tossed him over the shoulders of his own black horse.

"Can't leave you here, Bob," Shell said in a low voice. "Somebody'd sure as hell wonder. This way they'll probably figure you're downright unreliable, that you've wandered off for a drink or a woman. What do you think?"

Bob didn't feel like answering. The scarf crammed into his mouth might have had something to do with it.

Shelter turned and looked up the trail once more. Still silent, still dark. Then he heeled the black and guided it down the winding trail toward Crater which glittered dully like an unpolished jewel out on the black desert.

12

Crater was sleeping when Shell trailed in. A few lights burned in the hotel, and one in the back room of the saloon, reddened by the painted-out windows. Outside of that it was silent and dark.

Shelter had circled the town and come in from the west, looking things over carefully before he eased the black up a back alley, working toward Bert Quail's office, easily identified by the fresh sign: "Arizona Southern."

Behind the blacksmith shop which cornered the stables, Shell spotted a woodshed and he told Bob, "That'll be home for a while."

He walked the black up behind the shed where they were hidden in moon cast shadows and with a quick glance around he stepped down and dragged the outlaw from the horse.

The man hardly wriggled as Shell sat him down in the damp, spider-infested shed and bolted the door.

Shelter led the horse along the alley and tied it with a slip knot at the rail behind the emporium, close at hand.

Then, moving ghostlike through the shadows, he eased into the narrow space between the emporium and the saloon. From there he could just see the dark rear window of the new stage office—an office Quail just happened to share with the town's new female lawyer.

He crouched there, gun in hand, watching the road. The hours passed slowly and Shell's legs stiffened with the motionlessness. The pale moon grew smaller and drifted high in the Arizona sky.

Doubt had begun to creep into his thoughts. Suppose Quail had a house somewhere else and it was there Du Rose had gone? Suppose Du Rose had decided to wait until daylight. Suppose Guthrie had changed his mind and put hobbles on Du Rose?

The sound of an approaching horse chased all of those doubts aside. Shell tensed, eased forward slightly, and peered up the alleyway.

He held his breath, afraid to move. He did not want to chase this quarry off. He hadn't come three thousand miles to lose Charles Du Rose again.

Was it Du Rose? He strained his eyes trying to penetrate the deep shadows, uncertainty whirring in his brain until the man pulled up at the rear of the Arizona Southern office, dropped the reins to his bay and strode to the rear door where he gave three resounding raps.

Du Rose. Here.

And there he was. Shell decided he owed Sam Rutledge a drink. Du Rose threw back his head and whistled, looking to the second story of the building. There was no answer and he lifted his fist and pounded again, louder still on the unpainted door.

This time there was a response. The window upstairs was illuminated by pale, flickering lantern light and Shell heard grumbling. The window was thrown open and Shell withdrew into his recess, listening.

"Who is it?" The voice was Bert Quail's.

"Me," Du Rose answered.

"What the hell do you want?" Quail responded, his voice tight.

"Something's come up."

"Something—what?"

"You want me to shout it to the world? Open up, dammit, Quail."

Quail turned and muttered something to someone else and then hissed, "All right. Just a minute."

The window slammed down again and then it was silent in the alley for a long minute. Shelter could hear the sound of his own heart beating. There was an excitement in him. The sort of excitement a man feels when a long task is nearly completed, when he can taste the end of the trail.

He heard the back door squeal open on rusty hinges, heard Quail's muffled voice: "Come on in."

Quail's boots clacked against the wooden stoop and then were silenced as the door shut again. Shelter gave them five minutes and then, stiffly, he rose from his hiding place.

Inching into the alley, he looked around carefully. He had speculated that perhaps Guthrie would reconsider letting Du Rose come in alone; but there was no one about. A gray cat shot out from behind an empty packing crate and scuttled up the alleyway.

Shelter, stepping as softly as a cat himself, eased toward the lighted window of the stage office. He could hear agitated voices already, and as he lifted his hatless head above the sill he could see Quail waving a menacing finger at Du Rose who sat placidly in a leather chair watching the man.

Quail was red faced. "I won't stand for this kind of cheap blackmail, Du Rose!"

"Oh, you'll stand for it," the dark man said. "You'll stand for it if you want to run those stages of yours."

"We made a bargain!" Quail's face was crimson. Du Rose in response only shrugged.

From the corner of his eye Shelter now saw another figure in the room. Through the clouded glass of the window he could at first only discern that it was a woman. When she spoke he recognized her instantly from her cultured drawl.

"What is all this about?" Phoebe Strawn wanted to know.

"This vulture wants to hold us up for more money," Quail said in exasperation.

"Only a little more, Bert. A paltry amount compared to what the Camby Mine contract alone will pay you."

"He's got Guthrie talked into stringing along with him on this," Bert said, and Shelter saw Quail's eyebrow lift meaningfully. Du Rose missed the signal, but Phoebe didn't, and Shelter saw her moving toward the corner of the room.

Shelter had seen enough. He worked his way around to the back of the house, advanced lightly onto the rear step, and tried the door. The knob turned freely in his hand, and he opened the door, trying to suppress the protest of the rusty hinges.

Inside, he slid along the wall to the corner of the dark room which was being used as a storeroom. Beyond the wall Quail's voice rose in angry protest and dueled with that of Du Rose.

Shell inched across the floor, smothering a curse as a board squeaked underfoot. He had his Colt up and now he placed the flat of his hand against the door which was unlatched.

He could visualize it all quite clearly—step in, push them all into a corner, march them to the sheriff's office, enlist help, and round up Guthrie.

It wasn't to work that way. As Shell hesitated, a shot rang out in the other room. A roaring, large-caliber gun tore the silence of the house apart. Shell kicked the door open and burst into the room.

Du Rose was down. Sagged in the corner, his chest was smeared with crimson blood. Smoke still rolled in the room, stinging eyes and nostrils.

Quail was hunkered over Du Rose, a chrome Smith & Wesson .44 in his hand. He wasn't aware of Shelter's presence until Phoebe Strawn screamed.

Quail spun, his hand coming up, and Shelter triggered off. The roar of guns again filled the room, and Shelter felt a bullet tug at his sleeve, heard it slam into the wall behind him.

He stepped right, going into a crouch. The

smoke cleared and he saw Quail cowering against the floor, clutching his shoulder.

"Don't shoot, for God's sake! Don't shoot again."

It was then that the front door of Quail's house burst open and Snowden along with three citizens summoned by the shots crowded into the room where two men lay and Shelter Morgan, pistol in hand stood facing them.

"Drop it on the floor, Morgan," Snowden said, and there was authority in his voice. The shotgun in the lawman's hand carried even more authority, and after a moment's tense consideration, Shell nodded and opened his hand. The Colt clattered to the floor.

"Are you all right, Bert?" Snowden was crouched over Quail whose face was contorted with agony. His lips were drawn down hard, exposing yellowed teeth. He clutched his shoulder and rocked himself back and forth.

"What in hell happened here?" Snowden demanded.

"Him." Quail's finger lifted accusingly toward Shelter. "Busted in here and started shooting. Killed Du Rose."

"You son of a bitch!" Shell responded, a shadow of amusement in his voice. "You know damned well that's not what happened."

He started to step forward but two men grabbed him and threw him back. Shell had to admire the man's gall. Quail would try to bluff his way out of hell, most likely.

Then Shelter looked again and his mouth

formed itself into a bitter, straight line. The chrome pistol was gone. It wasn't in Quail's hand, and looking around he couldn't see it.

"He had a gun, Sheriff," Shelter said.

"Oh?" The sheriff glanced around as well. "Man says you had a gun, Bert."

"Damn liar," Quail said painfully. Snowden had unpeeled Quail's coat to examine the wound.

"You shot Du Rose," Shelter said savagely. "Where's the damned gun?"

"Where is it!" Quail snapped back through clenched teeth. His eyes were bright and mocking. "That's right, where is the gun, Morgan, if I had one? You broke in here and started shooting. That's all I know."

"You little bastard," Shelter said, losing his temper for the first time. "All you've got to do is ask her."

It was only then that he realized there was no one to ask. Phoebe Strawn was gone. She had disappeared in the excitement and there was no one at all to ask.

"Look for the gun, Sheriff! He had one, I'm telling you. Look and you'll find it."

"I'll look, Morgan." Snowden stood and faced Shelter—a hard, mustached sheriff who had seen more than his share of violence and didn't like looking at it any more. "I'll look, but I won't find it. Bert says he didn't have a gun, and I believe him. But I'll look, damn you, I'll look. Roy," he said turning to the nearest man, "lead Mr. Morgan over to our jailhouse and make him comfortable. Then find Judge Parker and tell him we've got us a murder."

"Find the woman," Shelter said. They had his arms clamped behind his back. Snowden turned a weary face to Shell.

"What woman?"

"The lawyer woman, Phoebe Strawn. She was here, Snowden, dammit. She saw it all."

"Bert?" the sheriff asked.

"I don't know what he's up to. Get me the damned doctor, will you?"

"He says there was a woman here, Phoebe Strawn."

"And he's crazy, I tell you. He's trying to confuse the issue. You think Miss Strawn was here at this time of the night? What do you think she is! Get me a doctor, Snowden, I'm bleeding to death."

"Search the house," Shelter said, "I'm telling you she was here, and she saw it all."

Snowden lifted his chin toward the back of the building and one of his deputies shuffled off to have a look. "Why'd you try to kill them, Morgan?"

Shell was silent, his blue eyes icy. "Find the woman," he repeated.

"She's not here, Morgan. Phoebe Strawn is not here. But I reckon there's a good chance you'll be seeing her again before long. Seeing as we've only got two lawyers in this town, I do believe there's every chance you'll be seeing her real soon. In court."

With that pronouncement and a dry chuckle, Snowden nodded to his men and Shelter was propelled across the room and out the door into

164

the cold night where a small group of men had gathered. They had hurried him out of that room, but there had been time. Time to see the triumphant smirk on Bert Quail's face, and if Shelter could have shaken free just then he would have kicked that expression right out of him.

The jail was stone, comprised of two cells and the sheriff's office separated by an adjoining door. Shelter was led in and thrown more roughly than was necessary into the cell which was cold, barren. Then the door slammed shut and he was alone in the darkness.

A blanket, precisely folded, nearly clean, lay on the bed which was supported by chains bracketed to the wall itself, and he slipped it over his shoulders.

Then, methodically, Shell went over the cell, testing windows, the door, the height, the heavy ceiling. It wasn't promising. The place had been built to last by a man who knew his stuff.

He sagged onto the cot, watching the stars through the iron-barred window. Now and then he heard gravel crunch beneath a boot. The alley was being guarded.

It was a bad spot and he knew it. He had no friends in this town but Ellie, and she was out trying to maintain a schedule of some sort, trying to rebuild the line. If she were here, she could do nothing. But it would have been a comfort.

Quail on the other hand was a solid citizen with friends everywhere. Besides that, he was a political contributor, meaning he had the sheriff in his pocket. And the judge? Probably him too.

Quail was a wealthy businessman, Shelter a drifter. It didn't take more than a glance to read the cards. Without Phoebe Strawn's testimony and the gun there was no hope at all of beating this. And in this territory that meant a quick trial, a quick sentence, and a quick neck-dance.

Restlessly Shelter rose and walked again to the window, gripping the cold iron bars with his hands. It was ironic—he had found Du Rose, had seen him die, and yet there was no satisfaction at all in knowing that the man had gotten what was coming to him.

For he was going to drag Shelter with him to the grave.

13

Dawn was yellow-bright. A mockingbird perched on the sill of the jail window scolded Shelter unmercifully for a moment before flying away to the freedom of the skies.

Shelter stared at the window for long minutes after the bird was gone, watching the sunlight stream into the room, the dust motes suspended in the sunbeams. It was a moment before it all came back to him. Crater, Arizona.

A murder suspect locked up and awaiting the executioner. He didn't doubt they were already building a scaffold, if they used such things in Crater, or scouting out a healthy cottonwood limb, since there was little doubt as to what the verdict would be. Or the sentence.

Again he paced the room, finding no chink, no hope for escape. Bert Quail must be laughing himself sick this morning. Well, maybe not with the bullet hole in his shoulder—but there would be other mornings, plenty of them to enjoy this little victory.

For Shell there wouldn't be so many more mornings.

At eight o'clock the deputy, unarmed, entered the hallway and slid a tray of food under the door, his eyes fixed cautiously on Shelter at all times. A second man with a scattergun stood in the door opening into the sheriff's office. They were taking no chances.

Shell picked up the tray and ate. It all tasted like unsalted dough—the eggs, the biscuits, the bacon. He chewed without thinking about it, and when he was through he shoved the tray under the door with his foot. The deputy who had been leaning against the wall, waiting, picked it up and trudged back out, the door banging shut heavily behind him.

At ten o'clock Snowden came in.

"Well, you're officially charged with murder," the sheriff told him from the other side of the iron-barred door. "The murder of one Charles Du Rose and the attempted murder of one Bert Quail."

Shelter just shook his head. It was hardly a surprise. He stood and circled the room as Snowden watched. Abruptly he stopped, leaning against the wall beside the window, arms folded.

"Look, Snowden, I don't know what kind of sheriff you are, but I can't believe you're the kind of man to let me hang for something I didn't do."

"No," Snowden said uneasily, "but Quail says you did it, and I wasn't there to see it differently."

"You didn't find the missing gun then? The chrome Smith & Wesson."

"We found no such thing," Snowden said, "and—you can believe it or not—but we went over

168

that place thoroughly. Under furniture, on the ground outside the window, up the chimney—no gun."

"You didn't find Phoebe Strawn either."

"Miss Strawn has apparently left town. There was a note on her bed in the boarding house where she was staying. Her mother had been taken ill in Baltimore, and Miss Strawn has gone back East to take care of her. The note was dated two days ago."

"That hardly proves anything."

"Neither does your story, Morgan." Snowden shook his head almost with regret, it seemed. "Unless you can come up with something else, son, you have got yourself a serious problem, a real serious problem."

That might have been understating it. If Shelter was feeling doubtful about his chances, the arrival of Tyler MacPherson at noon shattered the little that was left of his hopes.

The sallow-faced deputy unlocked the cell door and a small, spectacled man stepped reluctantly into Shelter's cell.

"What's this?" Shell asked. He was lying on his bunk, hands behind his head, watching.

"This here's Mr. Tyler MacPherson," the deputy announced. "Your counsel, as they say."

There was a sharp laugh and the deputy closed the iron door. MacPherson stood uncertainly in the center of the cell, glancing around apprehensively.

"You're my lawyer, is that right?" Shelter asked and at the sound of his voice the man jumped.

"Ah . . . yes," MacPherson finally answered.

"You see I'm the only lawyer in Crater just now. Judge Parker will prosecute you himself."

"Sounds fair," Morgan said dryly. MacPherson looked at him with vague puzzlement and then nodded slowly.

"Well," he waved his hand in a feeble gesture, "we have to make do."

"Yes." Shelter smiled despite himself. MacPherson was a narrow, faded man in an old and shiny suit. He had the mark of hard liquor on him. His eyes were bleary and his outsized nose was purple. He seemed to have the courage of a two-day-old cottontail. "I'm in good shape," Shell said with disgust.

"Well," MacPherson said hesitantly, sitting gingerly on the cot beside Shell, "we do seem to have rather a flimsy defense at this time." He opened his briefcase. Shelter reached over and gently closed it.

"MacPherson, none of this is going to help at all, and you and I both know it. I'm sure you'll do your best to represent me, but there's just no point in trying to build a defense when obviously there is none.

"If you want to help me," Shelter went on, "go out and find me a woman and a chrome .44 revolver."

With a show of reluctance, but also with obvious relief, MacPherson stood. Extending a hand which Shelter did not take, he backed to the cell door where he hollered for the deputy.

Shelter heard the door close, and then there was silence. Again the door opened as Shelter lay on the cot, eyes closed, and he thought MacPherson had returned.

"I really don't think you can help me," Shelter said with some irritation.

"I could," Ellie said, "but I don't think they allow it in jail."

He came to his feet and folded her into his arms. The deputy, obviously a romantic, stood outside watching, a grin on his face. "Private conversation, Bub," Shell said and the deputy vanished, whistling dryly.

"What's happened, Shelter?" Ellie asked with deep concern. "I was just ready to pull out on the Fort Thomas run when I heard my two passengers talking. They must have thought I was crazy when I leaped down from the box and high-tailed it over here."

"Sit down." Shell led her to the bunk, looking her over, admiring the fit of her jeans, the swell of her breasts beneath that habitual cotton shirt. Slowly then, without dramatizing it, he told her everything that had happened since leaving her. He gripped her hand.

"They'll hang you!" She came to her feet, still holding his hand. Her eyes were wide, her lower lip trembled. "This is awful. We've got to do something about it. Anything!"

"What, Ellie?" Shell asked mildly.

"I'll break you out of here!" she said with more enthusiasm than intelligence.

"There's only one way to help me—find Phoebe Strawn and drag her in."

"But she'd only lie, wouldn't she?"

"Probably. We won't know until we see her, will we? I'm sorry, Ellie. Sorry to put you through this."

"You're sorry!" Tears began to flood her eyes but she laughed, a broken, harsh laugh. "You're sorry—God, Shell, I'm the one who got you into this."

"And you'll get me out. Find Phoebe," he said, searching her eyes.

She sniffed, dabbing at her eyes with her shirt sleeve. "Where . . . I mean how? Oh, Shelter, I should have given this up a long time ago, you should have let me. I thought everything was looking up," she said, straightening herself. "I found a man to take Gila Junction, a driver—he drinks too much, I think, but . . . well, none of that matters, does it? I should never have tried to keep fighting."

"Maybe not. But we have to play the cards we've got now, Ellie." Shelter stood and he managed a smile for the dark-haired woman before him. "You get that coach rolling. It's a bad recommendation for Tanner, getting behind schedule."

"How can I worry about that? I was going to drive, but I'll get Ike—he's the driver I hired. Oh, Shell!" She fell into his arms. "I can't think, my head's a vast confusion. I'll have to rely on you, as always. What do I do? What?"

And Shell told her. Within half an hour Ike Byron, the new driver, had the stage rolling east and Ellie had begun her inquiries up and down the street, talking to the milliner, the boarding-house owner, the clerk at the bank. Meanwhile

172

Shelter sat in his cold, stony cell and waited, watching the shadows lengthen and change, watching time slowly run out.

The morning sky was still gray when they came for Shelter. Sheriff Snowden had a clean white shirt for Morgan to wear into "court," and the prisoner slipped into it.

They walked out into the streets of Crater as dawn was breaking, sending feeble incarnadine rays to pierce the low gray clouds which had gathered in the east.

There were groups of men, their breath steamy, the collars of their sheepskin coats up around their ears, watching as Snowden marched his hand-cuffed prisoner toward the 'Nother Round Saloon which was the courthouse on this bleak morning.

The bartender swept the porch, wearing an apron over his black suit. A top hat was perched on his round head. "Court's in session!" he hollered, cupping a hand to his mouth.

Behind Shelter half the town tramped toward the saloon, ready for a hanging, certain that they would not be denied one.

Shell was hauled in and seated on a cane chair. The tables were still stacked in one corner. The floor of the saloon had been washed down and covered with fresh sawdust. But despite that and the fact that the doors and windows all stood open, the room smelled of stale cigars and green beer, of cheap whiskey and cheaper women.

The judge entered a few minutes later, swept along by a crowd of eager well-wishers. The judge took up his position behind the bar. A languorous nude which hung on the wall behind him had been draped with canvas out of respect for the sober proceedings.

Shelter was flanked by two guards with badges and shotguns. His manacled hands lay on his lap. The judge eyed him with flat malevolence.

After a minute the crowd parted and, amid cheers and wishes for good luck, Bert Quail entered, his coat hung loosely across his shoulders, a tight new bandage evident beneath the shirt he wore.

As Shelter watched, Quail limped into the room—although his leg had not been injured—and nodded to the judge who smiled benignly in return. Snowden himself, standing at the end of the bar in a respectable brown suit, kept his expression empty as Quail walked past him.

On the heels of Quail came dozens of observers. Half the town crowded into the saloon; the air was alive with chatter and shouted greetings. Judge Parker, red-faced, stout, mustached, let it go on for fifteen minutes or so as he slowly studied the brief before him on the counter.

Then, as if awakening from a dream, the judge looked around and began furiously pounding on the bar with a gavel until the courtroom, such as it was, gradually fell silent.

"The People versus Shelter Morgan," the judge intoned. "Will the defendant rise?"

Shell did so, observing from the tail of his eye a frantic MacPherson rushing into the saloon, his eyes bloodshot, his tie askew.

Judge Parker glared at MacPherson and said, "Shelter Morgan, you are charged with killing one

174

Charles Du Rose, and with attempting to murder Bert Quail, here present, how do you plead?''

"Your Honor!" MacPherson waved a frantic hand. "The defense wishes to move for a postponement."

"Denied," the judge said as if ordering breakfast. "How do you plead, Morgan?"

"Does it matter?" Shell said sourly.

"I won't have you making a mockery of this court!"

"It's not me that's making it a mockery, Judge," Shelter said.

Parker was aching to cite him for contempt, but that didn't seem to make a lot of sense with a man who was about to be hanged. He contented himself with a lot of gavel-banging.

When the judge had worn himself out with that, he finally recognized MacPherson who was jumping around like a monkey on a stick. A quartet of cowboys in the back of the room were laughing themselves silly over the ways of Arizona law, and Shell guessed it was all amusing enough if your life wasn't hanging in the balance.

"Mr. MacPherson?" the judge said with gravity.

"Your Honor, we plead not guilty."

The judge nodded his head, eyes on MacPherson as if waiting for the lawyer to continue, but MacPherson was done. He sat beside Shell, offering his client one shaky smile.

"Due to the paucity of legal representation," Parker announced, "I will act as county prosecutor in this case, client already being provided with counsel."

That didn't even raise a murmur, and Shell

guessed it was old established practice in Crater for the judge to step from behind the bench, or bar as the case might be, and present his case to himself.

"Mr. Bert Quail!" Parker said in heavy, stentorian tones. "Step to the witness stand."

There was no witness stand, but someone slid a chair across the floor to the judge who hooked it on its way by and pointed at it. Quail, smirking, stepped to the chair and sat down.

"Now then." Parker paced the floor, hands behind his back. A cowboy burped and Parker shot him a steely glance.

"Wish they'd hang the man and open the damned bar," a voice behind Shell muttered.

"Mr. Quail," Judge Parker began, "tell us what happened night before last at your office."

"I got shot," Bert said lightly. That brought a trickle of laughter. Parker didn't smile. This law business was meant to be taken seriously.

"Yes . . ." Parker waved an encouraging hand; when Quail didn't continue Parker asked him exactly how all of this had happened.

"I was conducting a business meeting with my partner, Charles Du Rose."

"What sort of business?"

"We were considering trying to establish a stage line from Fort Thomas to Tucson, seeing as how the little girl who was trying to do it—"

"Ellie Tanner."

"Yes, that's right, Judge. Seeing as Ellie Tanner was just about to go bust. We thought there was an opportunity there for us."

"I see. When did Mr. Morgan make his appearance?"

"Oh, I don't know the time," Quail said easily, "but it was just as Du Rose was getting ready to leave. This Morgan busts in the back door and shouts: 'You bastards aren't going to take over the Tanner Line's route.' He worked for Tanner, you know."

"Yes."

"Well, he says that and I see he's got a gun, waving it all around. Then he looks at Du Rose and says, cold as ice, 'I've been waiting years for this chance, Du Rose,' and he cuts Charlie down."

The floor was given to MacPherson who gave it a valiant effort, but started off down the wrong trail and only made matters worse.

"Mr. Quail, why do you believe Morgan would try to attack you?"

"As I already said, he was working for the Tanner girl. He was out . . . eliminating competition."

"And Mr. Du Rose?" MacPherson pushed his spectacles up his nose. "Why in the world would my client kill Mr. Du Rose? You see, Quail, I am asking you what motive Mr. Morgan could have had."

"Ask Morgan," was all Quail would say.

Judge Parker did so when he got Shelter to the witness stand. He circled Shell a minute or so, his face going through a series of menacing contortions. Finally he stopped, stepped directly in front of Shell, and demanded: "Why did you come to Crater, Mr. Morgan? You are under oath, I remind you."

"I was looking for a man," Shelter responded.

"Yes. Your cousin, Amos Morgan." Parker

glanced at a paper he had left on the bar. "I ask you, under oath, Mr. Morgan—does such a man exist? Has Amos Morgan ever existed?"

"No."

The room buzzed, and Parker puffed up with satisfaction. The judge had him cornered and he knew it. The man positively glowed as he continued.

"But you did know Charles Du Rose."

"Yes."

"From when? When did you first meet him? The other night at Mr. Quail's home?"

"No," Shell admitted, "I knew Du Rose from a long time back."

"When, exactly?"

"I knew him during the war."

"What were your feelings toward Mr. Du Rose?"

"He was a low-life son of a bitch, and I felt contempt for him. He was a murderer and a coward, a black bastard." Shelter's eyes were sparkling. He knew he was saying the wrong things, but it didn't matter—they were going to hang him anyway. He told the story of the stolen gold, of Du Rose's treachery, of his part in the slaughter of some good men. And Parker let him tell it, let him dig his own grave.

When he was through Shelter thought he could detect sympathy on the faces of some of the men in the room, but all he had done, as he well knew, was to provide a strong motive for his having killed Du Rose.

"And so you hunted him down?"

"That's right."

"And killed the man."

178

"No." The room buzzed again. "I didn't shoot him. Du Rose was in partnership with Quail. He and Jeremiah Guthrie. Guthrie and Du Rose decided they wanted a bigger cut of the pay-off and—"

"This is sheer speculation, Mr. Morgan," Parker said with a laugh.

"The hell it is. I was on the Mesa Grande listening when they made the deal." That caused a few comments in the room—everyone there knew what it would take to ride boldly up onto the Mesa Grande. "And so I knew Du Rose was coming to see Quail. I followed him into the building and heard them argue. I heard shots, and when I busted in Du Rose was shot and dying. Bert Quail was standing over him with a chrome Smith & Wesson. And," he added, "a certain Phoebe Strawn was standing there watching it. If you can find her, she'll bear witness to it."

"But the sheriff found no chrome pistol, Mr. Morgan," Parker said mockingly.

"No. He didn't."

"Nor did he find Miss Strawn. Miss Strawn, in fact, had gone home to Baltimore the day before."

"No," Shelter argued, "she definitely did not do that. Because she was there, in that room, and she saw Bert Quail murder Charles Du Rose."

"That's your story." Parker nodded, pacing the floor, throwing up his arms in exasperation. "Although the prosecution has shown motive, opportunity, and has an eye witness. You are going to stick to that wild tale?"

"I've no choice, Judge. It's the cold, honest truth."

Parker, shaking his head, walked before the jury who sat in twelve front-row seats. He talked to them in a low, weary voice.

He explained the laws of evidence and then broke into a long, arm-waving diatribe against law breakers who held the sanctity of human life in contempt. The judge was good at it; Shelter had to give him credit. He liked to hear himself talk, but his mind was logical, his tongue sharp, and his manner persuasive. MacPherson could only sag in his chair, limp as a dish rag, his face glistening with perspiration. The man obviously wanted only to get this over with, then go home and crack the bottle of bourbon he had hidden there.

The verdict resulted from a minute's muttering between the men of the jury, and there was absolutely no doubt about what it would be. Shell figured, in their shoes he would have voted the same way. Still there was a haunting ring to the word.

"Guilty." The foreman looked at Shell, shrugged almost sympathetically, and sat down again.

"Is there anything else you wish to say, Mr. Morgan," the judge asked, "before sentence is passed?"

The voice from the rear of the saloon was loud and clear, and Shelter's head came around, a smile spreading across his broad lips.

"I don't know if Shelter Morgan's got anything else to say or not, Your Honor," Ellie Tanner said, hands on hips, her hat tipped back, "but I surely the hell do have something to say!"

180

15

The courtroom was thrown into an uproar. Someone laughed out loud, and Parker stared at the small, spunky girl who stood near the batwing doors to the saloon.

"Miss Tanner?"

"That's right, and I've got something to say, Judge Parker."

"I am sorry," the judge said formally, "but the trial is over and any further remarks are moot."

"Remarks, hell! I brought you something to look at. You tell me if it's important."

Then Ellie turned and called out through the doors, and a tall, whiskered man appeared, dragging behind him a well-dressed, but slightly rumpled woman.

Phoebe Strawn! Her hat was tipped over her eye. There was mud on her skirt, and it looked as if she had—by God, she *did* have a nicely developing black eye. Ellie looked smugly pleased.

"What is this? What in the world!" The judge banged his gavel, but the saloon didn't fall silent again until Ellie wanted to speak.

"This here is my new driver, Ike Byron. And this woman—well, you all know who she is. I asked Mr. Byron to keep his eyes open." Ellie turned and spoke directly to Shell. "She wasn't in town. I scoured it from one end to the other. So I sat down and thought, and I realized—hell! There's only one way out of Crater, isn't there? For a person who don't ride and doesn't even own a horse." Ellie's face was flushed. "She *had* to take the stage."

"Miss Tanner, I don't see—"

"You will, Judge," Ellie went on. "I told Mr. Byron to keep his eyes open on his eastbound run, and he did. Tell 'em what happened, Ike."

"I found this 'ere woman three mile down the line, settin' on a suitcase. She flagged me down, and recollectin' Miss Tanner's instructions, I just wheeled that coach around after this gal was aboard. She squalled like a wildcat all the way back, but the way I had that team runnin' wasn't nobody going to jump."

"She—" Phoebe Strawn spoke for the first time. She lifted a finger, pointing at Ellie Tanner. "She attacked me!"

Shelter glanced at Quail. He was having a tough time holding himself together. Snowden was frowning, sucking at his lip. The judge was annoyed—Ellie had broken up one of his best speeches.

"She tried to run," Ellie said, looking at the men in the room, men she had known since childhood. "I had to tackle her. Then," she turned around toward the bar where the judge stood. "I took her bag and found this."

She slapped the chrome Smith & Wesson on the bar and it glittered like a cold star, drawing all eyes to it. Ellie turned triumphantly, winked at Shelter, and sat down in a chair. "Now let her tell us about *that*," she concluded.

"Miss Tanner," the judge said as if speaking to a child, "I appreciate this effort and the remarkable coincidence it seems to substantiate—"

"Judge," Sheriff Snowden said, stepping forward. There was a determination in his face Shelter had not seen before. "We're all interested in justice around here. I know you are, sir. Let's hear what the woman has to say."

"Why . . ." Parker glanced around nervously. He was facing a room full of voters. "Of course, Sheriff Snowden. Of course. Miss Strawn," he said, his voice resuming its authority, "if you would be so kind as to be seated in the witness chair."

Quail was rigid in his chair. He shot a single, hard glance at Phoebe Strawn, but she shook her head and said, "What's the use, Bert? They know. What's the use of it?"

Then, after being sworn in, she sat in the chair, her hands smoothing the stained skirt she wore, eyes submissive, mouth set in surrender.

"I ran," she said. "I ran until I couldn't run anymore. The stage came along and I waved it down. He stopped and I felt relief. Until he turned and started racing back toward Crater. I screamed at him. I wanted to jump—but I would have broken my neck. For what? I asked myself that.

For what?

"When we reached Crater that girl—" she pointed shakily at Ellie—"leaped at me and . . . hit me in the eye." Someone laughed out loud in the back. "I knew it was a mistake. Knew it all the time."

"Miss Strawn," the judge said, not unkindly, "none of what you have told us has anything at all to do with the subject at hand: the matter of the death of Charles Du Rose. Have you any testimony which might bear upon the disposition of this case?"

"Oh, boy," she said. "Do I." She smiled a sickly smile at Bert Quail, wagged her head and asked: "Where do I begin? Sorry, Bert, I'm not going to be locked up for something you did."

Shelter had been watching Quail's eyes, and he saw the sudden panic there. Quail had been sweating and now, with Phoebe's last pronouncement, he gathered his muscles and started to spring from the chair.

Shelter started to move as well, but there was no need for it. Sheriff Snowden, his jaw set, clamped a hand on Quail's shoulder. "Sit, Bert," the sheriff said. "Let's hear the woman out, shall we?"

Parker, a man now slightly off balance, instructed Phoebe Strawn to tell what she knew about the incident. Phoebe, her head hung forward, her hat clinging precariously to her flame-red hair nodded.

"Du Rose came to the stage office. He asked Bert for more money."

"That's a lie, Phoebe!" Quail shouted.

"Shut up, Bert," Snowden said softly.

"Go on," Parker said.

"Yes," Phoebe licked her lips. "Du Rose said he and Jeremiah Guthrie wanted more money or else the Arizona Southern would have exactly the same trouble as the Tanner Line had. Bert told him to go to . . . Bert told him no, but Du Rose was persistent. And so," she shrugged, "Bert shot him. With that gun." She nodded toward the chrome Smith & Wesson which lay on the polished wood of the bar.

MacPherson, roused out of his lethargy got to his feet. Excitedly, he asked, "And where was Mr. Morgan at that time?"

"I can't say. In the kitchen? Outside the room, anyway. Then he came in and Bert tried to shoot him as well. Morgan shot Bert and he went down. In the smoke and excitement I was able to pick up the pistol and escape."

"And why did you do that, Miss Strawn?"

"Well, it's obvious, isn't it? With the pistol Bert Quail was going to hang. If the pistol was found . . . oh!" She was looking at the Smith & Wesson now and so was almost everyone in the room. "Sorry, Bert, but after all, what could I do?"

"You dirty little bitch," Quail said, his voice a low growl, his eyes fierce and animal. "You lousy, stinking bitch."

"Easy," Snowden said. "There's gentlemen in the room. Some of them might want to crack your skull for talk like that, Bert—and I might be one of them."

But they didn't want to crack his head—they wanted to hang him. They had come for an execution, and it looked like they weren't going to be disappointed. Parker, smooth as any politician, switched sides and went on with the speech about the responsibility of the law and its officers toward criminals.

Shelter only vaguely heard it. Ellie was next to him now, clinging to his shoulder, and he managed to smile for her, to kiss her once lightly. When he looked up again Quail was being led out, his shoulders drooping, his head hanging low. He said nothing more as he shuffled from the room, a deputy on each arm.

"Sorry, Morgan," Snowden said, and Shell almost believed he was.

"Get these off me." Shell held up his wrists and Snowden unlocked the handcuffs.

Shell rose and with Ellie at his side he walked out into the gray of morning. Thunderclouds were stacked high into the sky and a cold and threatening wind drifted dust, leaves, and litter along the street.

The stage driver was there and he apologized to Ellie. "Those passengers are mad as hell, ma'am. I don't expect they'll ever ride Tanner again."

"Don't you worry about them, Byron," she said. "Maybe they're mad at you, but you're in good standing with the boss. We can't thank you enough."

The tall men nodded shyly. "Well, guess I'll pack 'em up again and try for Fort Thomas." He glanced skyward. "Looks like we might have some wash-outs now."

As if confirming that guess the first large, spattering drops of rain began to fall. Byron touched his hat brim and was gone. They could see an older woman berating the stage driver, see him bow and apologize, then step into the box and whip the team out of Crater onto the eastbound road.

"Looks like you've found yourself a good one there, Ellie," Shell said.

"I think so." She looked up at him and smiled. "I've been lucky with men lately."

Shelter saw Snowden walking back toward his office, shoulders hunched against the rain which slanted down steadily now, and he said, "I've got to talk to Snowden, Ellie."

Before she could ask why, he was gone, striding across the street which was already turning to mud. Rain veiled the small, dirty town and Ellie. She took a deep breath, laughed out loud, and turned toward her tiny new office.

Going into the office, which was only a corner of the post office, she sat down and the smile fell away from her lips. She knew what Morgan was going to do—the kind of man he was, there was nothing else to do. But she also knew she couldn't argue him out of it and so she got to work, trying to figure some sort of schedule, considering the lack of horses, the condition of their stages, and the paucity of crew.

Once she looked up, pencil poised, to watch the rain wash down beyond the clouded window. She wondered just then who was crazier—herself or Morgan.

Morgan banged open the sheriff's office door and stepped in, tracking water and red mud across the floor. Snowden appeared from the cells, a key ring in his hand. He stopped, eyeing Shelter warily.

"What do you want?" Snowden asked. "I told you I was sorry, Morgan. What more can I do?"

"You can do what's right," Shell said. He sat down in the sheriff's chair, throwing his hat on the desk.

"What do you mean?" Snowden hung the key ring on a rusty hook on the wall and turned toward Shell.

"I mean the one who's been hurt by all of this is Ellie Tanner. She's the one who lost an uncle, she's the one who's nearly bankrupt. She'll fight on now, Snowden, but it won't do her a damned bit of good, will it? Not while Guthrie's still up on that mesa."

"What can I do?" Snowden began with a laugh which broke off as Shelter leaned suddenly forward, those icy blue eyes hard and dangerous.

"You can do what you should have done a long while ago. You can raise a posse and follow me up to Mesa Grande. Jeremiah Guthrie's up there. He's there because you didn't have the guts to go after him. And because you didn't, good men died. I think you owe it to Ellie Tanner, Snowden."

Snowden glared at Shell for a moment. Then he turned and walked to the open door, watching the silver rain drive down.

"It's raining today," he said.

"Yes, dammit!" Shelter slammed his hand down on the sheriff's desk. "And tomorrow it will be muddy, and the day after that it'll probably be dusty again! How long can this wait, Snowden? How many excuses can a man have?"

Ellie stretched her intertwined arms overhead and nodded with small satisfaction. There was just enough money, used judiciously, to see them through to the next scheduled gold shipment. After that Tanner would be back on firm footing.

Her thoughts were interrupted by a strange sound.

She rubbed her tired eyes and listened more intently. Something was up. Putting her pencil down she shoved her chair back and walked across to the door. She opened it in time to see the last of them.

They rode through the rain, a line of black men, ghostlike in the downpour. Men in black slickers and black hats, faceless, armed men, and they rode westward, toward the Mesa Grande.

She stood there for a moment, the wind pushing cold rain into the room, twisting her hair with icy fingers. Then the men were gone, swallowed up by the rain, and Ellie closed the door and returned to her desk where she lay her head on her arms and began to cry.

15

The water trickled from Shelter's hat brim. The desert was nearly invisible through the screen of heavy, cold rain. Low, jumbled clouds rolled past, racketing occasionally with deep-throated thunder. Flashes of bone-white lightning flared up, briefly illuminating the flats, but then, just as rapidly, darkness smothered the brilliant light. And suddenly there was nothing. Nothing but the wet horse beneath him, the cold and the wind.

It was a moment before he heard the voice above the roar of the rain, the whip and shriek of the wind. He glanced to his right to see Snowden yelling at him.

"You picked a hell of a day for it!"

Shelter only nodded, smiling thinly. He had picked a hell of a day, but at least he had picked one. Snowden had had his choice of a hundred days but he had found none of them suitable.

"They can't see us any better than we can see them!" Shell called back, and Snowden nodded.

It was true—Guthrie's men had held a nearly impregnable position, and a part of the reason for its security was the wide view they had of the desert flats. Today the Mesa Grande, shrouded in twisting black clouds, was not the fortress it had been yesterday.

Vision was cut off, communications were slowed, the conditions bad, and so there was a chance. Enough of a chance, Shelter judged. Snowden had his own opinions.

One thing worried Shelter. Guthrie undoubtedly knew by now that someone had penetrated his security—Bob had simply disappeared. That meant there would be more guards, more chance of ambush, though in this weather a sniper too was at a disadvantage. They would have to play it as it came.

Shelter shifted in the saddle, able to see only a handful of the fifteen men who traveled with him. He knew none of them, had no idea what they were capable of.

Most of them had been in the saloon courtroom, and had signed on out of a moment's fervor, out of pity for Ellie Tanner, perhaps. The rain was cooling that fervor quickly. The guns of Jeremiah Guthrie would quickly dampen what was left of it.

Now, through the parting clouds, Shelter had a glimpse of the dark, glistening bulk of the mesa itself. He leaned nearer to Snowden and shouted, "Let's veer south!"

The sheriff nodded, understanding. There was no point in approaching from straight on. What Shell had in mind was to get to the foot of the mesa some distance away from the trail and in that way approach unseen.

The water lay in steel puddles across the desert floor. The posse had to ford one arroyo, which, dry the day before, now roared with muddy water. That foiled another part of the plan—Shelter meant to keep to those washes where possible. The walls of the arroyos were high enough to hide an approaching horseman. Now they were impassable.

The clouds stayed low, offering protective cover, and the rain continued to lash down. Glancing around him Shelter saw sullen, uncertain faces. They were thinking the same thing every man entering battle thinks—it was a hell of a bad day to die.

The mesa, swathed in flat-bottomed clouds, loomed up suddenly before them and Shell halted, checking his guns. The others followed suit. A vagrant ray of sunlight gleamed on their rain-glossed slickers briefly before the clouds, tenacious and swift, smothered it.

Shell looked at Snowden, nodded, and led out.

The walls and the mesa, red, seeping rain water, rose high above Shell's left shoulder. He recognized the land around him now, knew the rimrock trail lay only a few hundred yards ahead.

His horse moved silently over the muddy earth, the wind pressed his slicker to his chest. Rain was cold in his face, his gun cool in his hand.

Shell suddenly found the opening and with a cautioning glance at Snowden, he led up. The weather, with them all day, obliged once more. The clouds came in low, smothering them in damp, cottony grayness.

Shelter peered through the cold rain, knowing where the guard post was—or had been. There was no reason to change it, but Guthrie might have, if he was a cautious man.

He wasn't that cautious, apparently. Shelter reined up abruptly, Snowden's horse nearly trampling on the heels of his own. Shell touched his nose and motioned for silence. Now Snowden too smelled the woodfire smoke in the air.

Shelter dismounted, leaving his long gun in the boot. Then he slipped into the rain-heavy brush and climbed the slope through the clouds and rain. He scrambled up a good two hundred feet, worked his way along the hillside and then crept down.

He could smell the smoke for a hundred feet, but he didn't see the guards until he was almost on top of them. Two rain-washed, unhappy men sat hunkered over a small, smoke fire. One of them spoke, but the downpour washed out his words.

Shelter didn't bother to speak. He stepped into their camp, his Colt leveled and the guards' hands went up. They watched with brooding eyes as Shelter walked to them, kicked their guns away, and whistled.

His whistle was answered, and in a matter of minutes Snowden and two members of the posse were in the camp. Swiftly they tied the outlaws, gagged them, and left them to soak in the rain.

The second guard post was even easier. Shell caught the man with his pants down. Literally. Crouched behind a rock, taking care of business, he was astonished to look up and see Morgan, gun in hand, perched on a rock.

"Finish up," Shell told him with a grin. "I'm not inhuman."

The gun seemed to make it impossible. The guard stood, buckled up his pants, and handed his gun over meekly.

"So much for the easy part," Shell said, wiping the rain from his eyes. "I don't think Jeremiah Guthrie will be taken down so easy."

"No," Snowden agreed. "Not since we've got him standing in the shadow of a noose." He smiled faintly at Morgan as the guard was tied up and left in the bushes. "You've got some Injun in you, ain't you?"

"It's been said," Shelter admitted.

They rode the trail until it was possible to get off it and take to the shelter of the timber. There they moved more silently, with greater security. Shelter knew the way and he led them to the low knoll where he had first seen Guthrie's camp.

"There he is," Shell said, and Snowden, peering through the rain, saw the two campfires, saw the four men posted as guards, saw the dozen who were gathered around the fire trying to fight off the chill of the bleak day.

"Fine. Now just how in hell do we take him?"

That was a question Shell had been giving consideration for some time. He thought he had the answer—hoped he did—and now with a wink he led Snowden and the posse over the ridge and through another stand of timber.

"There," Shell pointed. "I saw 'em first time up."

"What?" Snowden asked irritably. Looking into the valley he saw a string of outlaw horses standing close together. The drifting clouds revealed them and then closed again. "I don't see a damn thing but horses."

"That's all you're supposed to see," Shelter said with a wink. "That's all Guthrie's supposed to see. Let me tell you what I want to do."

Jeremiah Guthrie sat morosely by the smoky fire. The wood was wet, his clothes were wet. Everything was wet and he was sick of it. Caleb Guthrie sat next to his father, but he didn't speak. He could read the black mood in Jeremiah's eyes.

"Where is the bastard?" Jeremiah wondered out loud for the fiftieth time.

"Probably waitin' for the rain to let up."

"He had time to get back before it even started. He was just going to see Quail and come right back."

"Think he pulled out on us?" Caleb asked and Jeremiah's scowl deepened. "Nah," Caleb said, "why would he?"

"Why!" Jeremiah threw his tin cup into the fire—the coffee was cold, half rain water. The cup drew sparks, the fire spat steam briefly. "Damn that Du Rose! If he did—"

"Hell, why would he?" Caleb repeated. A smaller, narrower version of Jeremiah Guthrie, he was still cowed by his old man although he was on the far side of thirty.

"Use your damn brain, boy!" Jeremiah muttered. "He used me. Shook Quail down for more money, pocketed it and rode out whistlin'."

Lightning flashed in the skies and Caleb involuntarily looked skyward. The men across the fire had been listening without seeming to and their misery deepened. When a man figured sitting around on this forsaken, cold mesa was leading to a bigger payday, it was all right. When you were just sitting—well, that was a different story.

"Now what?" Jeremiah grumbled and Caleb turned his head as well.

"How in hell . . ."

Their remuda of horses was walking slowly across the valley, grazing as it went.

"Who in hell was watching them horses!" Jeremiah thundered.

"Carl."

"I'll beat his damned head in," Jeremiah promised. The horses drifted nearer the camp, slick with rain, moving slowly through the low cloud cover. "Get some men, round them up, Caleb."

"Yes, sir." Caleb started to rise, froze his motion as he stared in disbelief and then sat down again. "Jeremiah!" he said hoarsely.

"What in hell's the matter with you?"

Caleb didn't get the chance to answer, to tell his old man that each of their horses had grown another two legs, that each of those legs was wearing pants.

At some unseen signal the posse members halted the horse each had been walking and, laying their guns across the animals' backs, they opened up.

196

The camp was thrown into vast, deadly confusion. Bullets whined through the air, kicking sparks from the fire, puncturing canteens, piercing flesh and bone. Jeremiah Guthrie dove for his rifle and came up firing. The posse, nearly on top of the camp had killed three of Guthrie's men before anyone could react. Now Guthrie reacted. With savage anger he levered six shots through his Winchester as the rain washed his scant hair across his eyes—and as Caleb lay writhing on the ground beside him, clutching at his arm which had been torn open by hot, jagged lead.

The horses had taken off in mad panic and that left the posse open to return fire. Jeremiah grunted with satisfaction as a man in a black slicker tumbled to the ground, dead.

But Guthrie's situation was desperate and he knew it. Falling back, firing his Winchester until the magazine was empty, he watched his men dying all around him. *Out*—there had to be a way out; there always had been throughout his long career as an outlaw, and now opportunity presented itself.

A wide-eyed roan horse ran through the heart of the camp, scattering the fighting men, and headed directly at Jeremiah. He braced himself, and when the roan was abreast, he grabbed for the mane.

It nearly yanked his shoulder from its socket, but he caught and held the mane. Then with a dozen long, clumsy strides, bullets winging around his head, he managed to throw a stocky leg up and over the roan's back. In moments he was pounding away from the camp, leaning low across the horse's withers, riding for the safety of the pine woods.

Shelter had popped up from behind his shielding horse and fired first at Caleb and then at Jeremiah Guthrie. Caleb he had tagged hard, but then the horse in front of him had joined the harried stampede and his next shots had been haphazard, taken between the wildly running horses.

The first volley, its surprise complete, had taken down half of the Guthrie men, but now it was a bloody, hectic gunfight. Shelter rushed for the camp, saw a man loom up before him from out of the thick clouds, and he fired pointblank, watching the outlaw jerk backward as if a mule had kicked him in the chest. Vaulting that raider, he had entered the camp proper, seen with one quick survey that Caleb was out of it and that Guthrie was gone.

Racing on he was met by a hail of bullets from Guthrie's rifle. Shelter hit the ground, firing as he dropped, but the shots were wide.

He saw the horse racing past him, saw Guthrie reach out desperately and grab the roan's mane, saw the outlaw leader swing onto its back and disappear into the milky fog.

Shelter looked behind him and saw that Snowden had things well in hand. Already four outlaws were lying face down on the ground, hands behind their necks, beaten.

There was a wall-eyed blue roan nervously trotting near Shelter. He tried to halt it, missed, and cursed as the roan snorted and shied away.

A stocky bay with two white stockings was more tractable. It watched Shell with a wary eye, its nostrils flared, muscles quivering, but it allowed Shell to put a hand on its neck and let him slip onto its back.

Shell kneed it forward, his hand wound in the mane. He could no longer see Guthrie. The clouds were low, the rain heavy once more.

Guthrie's tracks, however, were still clear, and Shelter could follow them at a canter. Ahead the forest rose up from out of the gray-white gloom, and he rode that way, urging the horse on.

He was within a hundred yards of the pines when the rifle barked. Shell went low across the withers and pulled the little bay hard to the left, then to the right, zigzagging toward the timber.

Two more rifle shots flew wide, one by bare inches, and then Shell was into the pine woods. He dropped from the bay's back, letting the worried horse run on by itself.

Shell slipped behind a huge pine, shed his encumbering slicker and began cautiously moving through the woods. Water dripped heavily from the trees. The earth underfoot was sodden, slick. The tips of the pines were lost in the clouds and the day was dark, the wind shrieking through the forest.

His flannel shirt was plastered to his body and he began to shiver. He hardly thought about that, hardly felt the discomfort. His eyes were ablaze with a hunter's gleam. He wanted this man, wanted him bad.

It was Guthrie who had killed Willie Tanner. It

was Guthrie who had killed Mel Giles. It was Guthrie who had killed that gentle old woman and her husband. He had killed and burned and looted, and if he survived this day he would no doubt continue his violent ways.

Something had gone wrong with the man who was Jeremiah Guthrie. Somewhere along the line a hand had been too soft or too firm, he had been praised too much or damned too roughly.

But he was a grown man now, responsible for his own actions—and he had chosen crime, chosen to maim and injure. Shelter knew there was only one way to cure a killer like Guthrie. And he knew it was up to him to do it.

The rifle shot echoed through the timber, and Shell went to his belly as the .44-40 slug ripped the bark from the pine beside him.

He rolled downhill, into a gulley where a trickle of run-off flowed. Dashing to the rim of the gulley he saw, briefly, a dark, shadowy figure darting through the clouds—and he fired twice, his Colt held in both hands.

Guthrie grunted, went to a knee, fired wildly back, and ran on, holding his left hip with his hand.

Shelter was up out of the gulley himself, winding through the pines. Trees appeared and disappeared magically from out of the clouds and rain. The day had gone incredibly cold; the wind howled through the pines, covering all sound.

Guthrie was suddenly there, directly in front of him. Shell saw the kneeling figure of the man, saw the Winchester at Guthrie's shoulder—and he flung himself to one side.

But it was too late. The searing pain of a bullet tore at his shoulder. Shelter was spun around and he slammed against the earth, crawling desperately for the shelter of a jumble of rain-glossed gray boulders. A second shot was fired and a third, and Shelter answered to let Guthrie know he still had teeth.

Yet he knew he was in trouble. Sagging against a rock, tearing his sleeve open, Shelter saw the flood of crimson streaming down his arm, life flowing out of him.

Angrily he tied the wound up, using his teeth to help knot the torn shirtsleeve he used as a bandage. It was not enough. The blood was hardly slowed.

Shelter threw his head back, taking a deep, painful breath of cold air. The rain fell into his face. The world was cold, everything frozen except for the focus of white-hot pain which was the jagged wound in his shoulder.

"Guthrie!" he called. "Give it up! You can't get off the mesa, and you know it."

That didn't work. A hail of lead ricocheted off the boulders, deadly missiles seeking Shelter from out of the forest. He rolled away, crawled into the timber, and lay panting, his eyes studying the trees through a matrix of red and yellow, pain-inspired dots.

He clawed his way upslope, feeling the strength drain out of his body, feeling the cold seep into his bones and weary muscles, overwhelming him, chilling him to lethargy. His cheek was lying against the damp brown pine needles; his hands clenched and unclenched. He was gazing with fascination at the blue Colt in his right hand, at the waterspots on the barrel, the curve of the heavy hammer which somehow seemed new and mysterious.

Dammit, Morgan, snap out of it! He shook his head, realizing that the loss of blood was beginning to tell. There was a killing man out there, a man with a rifle, and he was stalking Shelter. Weary or not, injured or not, it was no time to quit. Shelter had been across the deserts, he had been winter-bound in the high up mountains, he had faced the Apache and the Kiowa, but he had never quit.

Now, just now, he felt like doing just that. No matter that the small insistent voice in the back of his skull urged him to rise, to come alert, to fight back.

Get up!

Why? He lay there, the rain falling down, running off his face, soaking his clothes. Because there is a job not done, because there must be more killing? Because some of those murderers from Georgia still lived, still prospered, still sat smugly in their houses on this night, houses paid for with blood money?

A procession of dead, ugly faces flashed before his mind's eye. Wakefield, Twyner, Bowlen, Chambers, Plum . . . all mocking demons now. Fainer, dead by his own hand, Custis burned alive, cursing from out of the crimson flames. Leland Mason, Roland Blue. Benton Gray!

Shell felt a hot tear in his eye and he blinked it away in annoyance. Pickett, Du Rose! All dead. Shelter was a man who lived to kill. A dark angel of retribution. Blood stained his hands.

Get up!

For what? Rise up and kill again. Fight again, be hurt again . . . his head swam with it. He could think of no reason to rise, to stop the slow seeping of the blood.

And suddenly she was there. Small, warm, trusting. Ellie Tanner was in his thoughts. He saw her face looking into his coffin, saw the silver tears in her eyes, felt the press of her breasts against his warm chest.

"Don't die, Shelter Morgan," her voice said from out of the cold mist. *"I want you with me."*

He pawed at the ground, knowing he could not let her down. He shoved out with his left hand, lifting his pain-racked body from the ground. Pine needles clung to his shirt, to his face. The pain was overwhelming, but he continued. Turning himself, he got to a sitting posture. His dark hair hung in his eyes. The rain beat down across his back. The Colt lay inertly in his hand and Jeremiah Guthrie stood triumphantly over him, rifle to his shoulder.

"So long, lawman," the outlaw growled and Shell saw his thick finger tightening on the blue trigger of the Winchester.

16

Jeremiah Guthrie stood there, a dark and bulky form against the background of timber and clouds. The rain drove down and thunder rumbled across the mesa. Guthrie had his Winchester to his shoulder and there was no way he was going to miss at that distance. No way in this world.

"Good-bye lawman," Guthrie said, and Shelter saw his eyes narrow, saw the small movement of his trigger finger.

Shell, watching it all, was numbed by cold, his thoughts dulled by his wound. Then suddenly white hot rage swept through him, freeing him from his frozen inaction. He thought, without framing his thoughts in words, of those who had died because of Guthrie, of those who would die in the future. He thought—all in the fleeting split-second he was allowed—of Willie Tanner, and of Ellie who was waiting, waiting. . . .

Shell's Colt came up and bucked in his hand. He thumbed the hammer back again and again, firing until the gun was empty and smoke formed clouds to rival those of the storm. Until his nostrils burned with acrid gunpowder smoke, until the thunder of his gun equaled that of the cloudburst, until the hammer fell again and again on empty chambers.

Guthrie had fired, must have fired, and he could not have missed. Why then was he lying flat on his face, punctured by Shell's bullets? Why then was Shell still able to think, to move?

Guthrie had missed as Shell's bullets cut him down. His slack form lay against the earth, sodden and cold. Shelter blinked away the smoke. It was like emerging from a dream.

Bracing himself against the boulder behind him he stood and then fell, the blood flowing from his shoulder, the day spinning madly, becoming black clouds and crimson blood, brilliant red and yellow stars and deep, deep silence.

Shelter slept, or he thought he was sleeping. Then he dreamed. Guthrie seemed to rise off the ground, brush himself off, smile, and say it was all a fine joke.

Then, shouldering Shelter, Guthrie walked to a horse, threw him over the saddle, and led him down onto the rain-swept desert, escorted by a dozen men in black monks' cowls. A gust of wind swept back the hoods from the men's faces and Shelter saw without surprise that they were blank, grinning skulls' heads.

Then for a while there was nothing but the rain, an iron-hard rain which seemed even to wash away the fiery pain, to wash away the desert and all of the earth, to cleanse sins and excesses of mankind. There was only rain, and it was a hard, judging rain. It fell and the world was washed away, and consciousness was gone.

It seemed to rain for days, for weeks. From time to time Shelter would open his eyes and he would think he was on a bed, watching sunlight through the curtains, and then the rain would come again, hammering him to gray-black unconsciousness.

It stormed for a week, a year, forever—and there were only tiny gaps in the endless storm. There would come a moment of silence and through it a smile would float, a soft touch, a delicate scent. But the rain always returned.

One day it did not.

One day Shelter awoke and he saw the sunlight through the window and knew it was real, that the rain had ceased. And when the door opened she stood there in a soft, blue gingham dress, her hair shining in the sunlight, her mouth lifted in an expression of surprise and hope and pleasure, and Shelter stretched out his hands to Ellie who crossed the room and lay her face against his chest, clinging to him.

And the rain was gone.

YOU WILL ALSO WANT TO READ . . .